Wakefield

OLD YANCONIAN DAZE

Bill 'Swampy' Marsh is an award-winning writer of stories, plays and songs. He grew up in a tiny town in south-west New South Wales and attended Yanco Agricultural High School. After backpacking through three continents and working in the public and private sectors, his writing hobby blossomed into a career. Bill's first collection of short stories, *Beckom (Pop. 64)*, was published in 1988. His stories feature regularly on radio, and his songs and plays have been performed across Australia.

By the same author

SHORT STORIES
Beckom (Pop. 64)

PLAYS
What The Crow Saw
River
1 . . . 2 . . . 3 . . . Pick it Up
Taking Flight . . . Takes it Off
The Garbage Twins, to the Rescue?

For Allan, Judy Lucy and Amy, A few short stories from my cousin's pen and in appreciation Yours aye Bill.
27.4.1996

OLD YANCONIAN DAZE

BILL *'Swampy'* MARSH

With best wishes.
Bill "Swampy" Marsh
Mar '96

Wakefield Press

Wakefield Press
Box 2266
Kent Town
South Australia 5071

First published 1995
Reprinted 1995

Copyright © Bill Marsh, 1995

All rights reserved. This book is copyright.
Apart from any fair dealing for the purposes
of private study, research, criticism or review,
as permitted under the Copyright Act, no part
may be reproduced without written permission.
Enquiries should be addressed to the publisher.

Cover photograph by Chris Carter
Book designed and typeset by Michael Deves
Printed and bound by Hyde Park Press, Adelaide

National Library of Australia
Cataloguing-in-publication entry

Marsh, Bill, 1950– .
Old Yanconian daze.

ISBN 1 86254 351 8.

I. Title.

A823.3

*To my loving sisters,
Barbara and Margaret*

Author's note

I would like to thank: the Old Yanconians' Union for its support; David and Christine Harris for their faith and editorial advice, which made this book a reality; the Coronary Care and allied units of Royal Adelaide Hospital who gave me the chance to complete this book and, I hope, many more; Margaret and James Holdsworth for having to live with the writing demons that drive me; Russ Elwin for his bright ideas; Lynn Hill for his computing (and musical) expertise; Jack Connell for his deft recording of my stories for radio; those many friends and family who were pillars of support when death came 'a knockin'; Bill Rawson; Chris Carter and his lightning lens; and the Writers' Centre (SA) of which I am a proud board member.

'Paris, France' won First Prize in the Dandenongs Short Story Literary Competition run by Papyrus Publishing 1993. 'A Night At The Oscars' won First Prize in the Flinders News Prose Award 1994. 'The Herb' received a Highly Commended Award in the Ararat Golden Gate Literary Competition 1992.

The writing of this book was assisted by the South Australian Government through the Department for the Arts and Cultural Development.

I would like to remind parents of prospective students of Yanco Agricultural High School that initiations and the privilege system are no longer part of the social structure. The school is now co-educational.

Contents

Five Star Welcome	1
Away in a Manger	9
Mister Swift and His Little Red PMG Van	15
Howling Chorus	19
The Portrait	22
'Ranting' O'Reilly	26
In the Swim	29
Paradise Lost	34
Einstein	38
Miracle Man	41
The Herb	46
Cookie	49
'Galah' Day	56
Well Above the Average	66
The Shadows of 'Dangerous Des' and 'Gorilla' Crowley	69
Bread and Jam	71
A Trip into Town	75
'Legs', the 'Chaff Cutter' and 'the flicks'	81
A Rough and Ready Mob	86
Hollywood Bound	89

Old Bandy	94
In the Wake of 'Horny' Jones	99
Our Gang	102
Ape	109
The Once-a-Term School Dance	112
A Night at the Oscars	119
The Twenty Per Cent Factor	123
The School Choir	127
She	132
Paris, France	135
Muck-up Day	140
Custer's Last Stand	145
Empty Pockets	150

'As you sow, so shall you reap'

Five Star Welcome

I was frightened, the day I arrived at Yanco Agricultural High School. It was one of those days when you know your whole life is about to change and nothing can be done about it.

Behind me lay my home town of Beckom (Pop. 64). A simple bush existence filled with friends of a lifetime, their laughter and grumbles, the warm security their presence held; smells so familiar you only missed them when they weren't wrapped around you like a comforting cotton ball of aroma. A place where my parents had been just a shout away. Yet now, at the grand old age of eleven years and eight months, I suddenly feared they had jettisoned me prematurely, into the vast unknown of my future.

There were six of us gathered on Yanco Railway Station that stinking hot day. All of us had come from the sticks; from farming regions throughout the south west and western regions of New South Wales, just raw bush kids really, flung together as if we were spare parts from an under-twelves jumble sale.

We milled around the station checking each other over until a small Bedford truck came to pick us up. The tray of the truck was surrounded by a reinforced wire cage and stunk like it had just come from the saleyards. We picked up our cases and ran toward the driver's cab to get the most comfortable ride.

'In the bloody back youse blokes,' a gruff voice barked out at us from inside the cab. 'Who do ya think ya are, a mob'a bloody Lord-High-'n-Mightys or somethin'?'

We turned in our tracks and sauntered around to the back of the truck. One kid clambered up onto the cage and opened the wire gate.

'Welcome aboard. The name's John Ashton,' the kid said as he helped each of us up onto the back of the mucky truck.

After we had jammed ourselves and our luggage into the cage, John slammed the gate, yelled out 'Take 'er away mate' and we set off on the last leg of our journey, the five miles to school.

As we were driven out of Yanco, I, along with the others, pushed my way to the back of the truck. There we gripped onto the wire cage for support, watching the township disappear. When I finally turned around again, John had made himself comfortable out of the wind, behind the cab. Drawn by his confident manner I went and squeezed myself in beside him.

'G'day, I'm Bill,' I said.

John shook my hand. He told me that he had a brother who had attended Yanco Ag during the Second World War. He reckoned that everyone at school went by nicknames, and he asked to be named 'Jug Ears' or 'Jug', as that's what his brother, Joe, had been called. They were keen for the family tradition to continue. He asked if I had a nickname. I told him it was 'Swampy', because my last name was Marsh.

Jug seemed armed with a wealth of information, passed on to him by Joe, about what lay ahead.

'Fer starters,' Jug announced with a loud voice of authority so that we could all hear him, 'the economy'a Yanco Ag runs on cigarettes, "herbs" as they're called. Money ain't worth a brass razoo 'cept fer buyin' ya herb stash.'

Then he told us about 'Dad-ak', the Headmaster. 'Me brotha Joe reckons that Dad-ak locks kids who muck up in the dungeon under McCaughey House and forces 'em ta live on bread, water 'n rats for weeks on end. Joe says he rules the school with an iron fist and a huge bunch of keys.'

''N steer clear'a "Ape", the Ag teacher. He once gave Joe such a canin' that 'is fingers came out lookin' like they been through a sausage mincer.'

Someone in our group must have looked doubtful because Jug quickly added, 'No joke mate. 'E's still got the scars. 'E's showed me.'

'And youse ought to know about how privileges work,' Jug continued, now that he'd grabbed our attention. 'That's where anyone can order us First Years about. We'll 'ave ta make way in line fer anyone senior. They can make us clean their shoes. They can bot our lollies, "chews" as they're called. 'N if they tell ya to do somethin', do it, else you'll be in big strife.'

Jug explained that the higher the year you were in, the more kids you held privileges over. Then in your final year, if you became a School Captain or a Prefect, you could roll the cuffs of your shorts up three times, give the strap to students who were 'insolent' or tried to buck the system and rule their lives with as much authority as Dad-ak or the 'Nits', as teachers were named.

As First Years, Jug said, we weren't allowed any privileges. 'Us First Years are called "Grots", 'cause a grot is dirty, ugly 'n useless.'

Then there were the initiation ceremonies performed by the Second Years. Jug told us to expect to be given the 'Royal Flush', which was where we'd have our heads shoved down a toilet and the chain pulled. He warned that if we kicked up a stink during our Royal Flushing we'd be forced to do unspeakable things. Things that he said Joe had told him were too frightening to mention.

I was beginning to wonder about this brother of Jug's, and if perhaps he had invented these stories just to put the wind up Jug. I couldn't be sure. They were certainly putting the wind up me. It sounded more like we were going off to live with some barbaric African tribe than to a bush boarding school. But by the look in Jug's eyes when he spoke and his graphic hand actions, I had the dreadful feeling that he, for one, believed every word of it to be true.

'Me brotha Joe says that when 'e wuz in First Year one kid got so homesick 'e hung 'imself in the showers of McCaughey House. They found 'im next mornin' danglin' by 'is school tie. All blue he was, with 'is eyes bulgin' out like light bulbs 'n 'is tongue hangin' a foot out'a 'is mouth.'

We reached toward our crisp blue-and-gold striped school ties and loosened them. But there was no relief. Jug immediately followed on with the macabre story about the bloke who jumped off the second floor veranda, fracturing his skull and breaking his arms and legs.

'Then there's the ghost who lives in McCaughey House, 'n on a full moon 'e's been know'd ta murder First Years while they're sleepin' in their dorms. Why, Joe woke up one mornin' 'n the bloke in the bed next ta 'im 'ad a meat cleaver stuck right through 'is noggin 'n a couple'a yards'a hose wrapped around his throat fer good measure.'

We gasped in terror and morbid fascination.

'Dead as a maggot 'e was,' Jug added, shaking his head almost in disbelief at his brother's story. 'Dead as a bloody maggot, Joe reckons.'

As we passed through the wrought iron gates at the school's entrance, displaying its sign – YANCO A RICULTURAL HIGH SC OOL – an emptiness came over me as if my body had been sucked of its blood.

'It's like a prison,' someone muttered.

To me, it was like entering a completely different world. The comforting summer browns, oranges and yellows I'd grown up with had disappeared. There were no towering concrete silos, which were the landmark of Beckom. I was completely swallowed up by dense river gum bushland. There wasn't a hint of dust in the air, only the sickly scent of damp earth and muddy bark.

Up the gravel drive we were transported, trapped together on the back of the truck, a small flock of blue-and-gold school uniforms . . . lambs to the slaughter. I had visions of being locked away forever; of never being allowed to see my parents again; of never seeing the outside world again.

'You all right?' Jug asked.

'I'm a bit scared,' I answered.

'We'll be okay,' he replied. 'We jus' gotta look after each other, that's all.'

After what Jug had told us, I fully expected to see kids living in an encampment of grass huts and dressed like natives, with big boiling cauldrons waiting to stew us up. But when we drove out of the thick bush I could hardly believe my eyes. With a clang of the truck's caged gates we were unloaded outside the main entrance of McCaughey House.

It seemed exactly as the school's brochure had said. The manicured lawns and picturesque gardens lay before us. The collection of rare and ornate roses formed a pathway down to the man-made lake. Willow trees lazily dangled their finger-like foliage into the lake's muddy waters. Three massive pine trees guarded an arched wooden bridge which stretched over to the main islet in the centre of the lake.

I turned to take in McCaughey House. It was the largest building I'd ever seen, almost like a brick-and-sandstone castle. The ground floor was curtained by huge arches. Behind them were large windows encased in thick wooden frames. I squinted up at the second story veranda and felt dizzy imagining a naked body, scorched with strap marks, falling in a flail of arms, legs and cries of desperation and homesickness.

'Youse the new Grots?' came a snaky voice.

Lowering my eyes I found we were being surrounded by a mob of blokes dressed in the school's day clothing of khaki shirts, shorts, socks and sandals. As one, we grabbed our suitcases and shuffled into a loose huddle.

'Look like a piss-weak bunch'a poofs ta me,' said another voice.

This brought a touch of ironic laughter from the growing khaki forces. We said nothing, only closed ranks.

'Hey you. You got shit all over ya precious school uniform,' said a bloke who had the cuffs of his shorts rolled up.

We searched amongst ourselves for the accused.

It was me.

'Hey Thommo, wha'da we do with a Grot who shits his school uniform?'

Thommo stepped forward and announced himself as Arthur

Thompson, the School Captain. He wasn't as rugged looking as the rest. He was tall and slight with snowy hair and rosy cheeks. I tried to explain that the mess had come from the sheep who'd been in the truck before us. Thommo completely ignored me and barked a decree to the khaki troops that anyone who soiled their sacred school uniform deserved to be taken to the lake and given a thorough dumping and washing.

Amid the cannibalistic cheers that these words brought, Thommo called, 'Go sick 'im Rags,' and a kid not much older than me shot out from the pack like a starving dog. He grabbed me by the tie and dragged me away from my group.

'The name's Rags Kelly,' he hissed.

I tried to recall if I'd ever stood in front of such a large group. I remembered the previous year's inter-school sports carnival at Temora when I won the hop, step and jump, after most of the opposition had been disqualified for getting their hops mixed up with their steps and jumps.

That Temora crowd had looked bored and lethargic. This mob was different. They looked wild and mean and restless. Their eyes burned for action. I stood before them, clutching my brand new Globite suitcase, terrified.

'You touch 'im 'n you'll 'ave ta deal with the rest of us,' came a voice from our group.

It was Jug Ashton. His brave words were supported by a couple of unenthusiastic, half grunted whispers.

Rags Kelly dropped his stranglehold on my tie and lunged toward Jug. As he did, I instinctively spun around and clocked him one over the back of his head with my suitcase.

The brawl erupted on the gravel outside McCaughey House. It rampaged onto the manicured lawns. Suitcases were flung and torn, and exploded into loose balls of clothing. The tempest ploughed into the picturesque gardens. It rioted over the rare and ornate collection of rose beds. It cascaded toward the man-made lake.

All became a frenzied blur. The background echoed with the blood-curdling chant of 'Fight! Fight! Fight!' At anything resembling khaki I took a wild swing. At anything resembling a school uniform I shouted encouragement. Then I was in the water. Someone was jumping on me. Someone was pushing my head under. My aching arms kept swinging like windmill blades gone crazy. Suddenly, a deathly silence enshrouded me. I lay there floating head down in the lake, with no one pushing me, no one jumping on me.

Even without looking, I knew Dad-ak was standing on the bank above. He had an eerie presence the like I'd never felt before. I tried to keep my head under the water, hoping he'd go away.

But I ran out of breath.

Jug had described him to a tee. Dad-ak stood short and squat like a dictator from one of Dad's war books. His brown beady eyes glared down at me. His stumpy fingers held the largest set of keys I'd ever seen. Keys that were made to fit every kind of lock imaginable, including dungeon locks.

Beside Dad-ak stood Arthur Thompson. A self-satisfied smirk was plastered over his dial. My friends, saturated to the bone in their ragged and ripped school uniforms, were slumped on the lake's grassy bank. The khaki army hovered in the distance like a circling pack of dingos.

'That's 'im, Sir,' Arthur Thompson pointed down at me. 'That's the bloke who started it all. Whacked poor Rags Kelly clean over the back'a the scone with 'is suitcase 'e did, Sir.'

'To my office, boys!' Dad-ak spat down at us and spun around, striding back toward McCaughey House. His piston-shaped legs pounded over the debris of loose clothing, shredded suitcases and uprooted roses. We stumbled along behind, attempting to pick up our belongings.

Into McCaughey House we poured, chasing the high-pitched ring of jangling keys. At the top of a double staircase a brilliant, leadlight collage of a shepherdess tending her sheep caught my eye. We slushed our way into the office and shuffled into a line in front of Dad-ak's desk. He examined us one by one.

Then he got to me.

'In all my years at this school,' he finally spoke. 'I've never witnessed anything as disgraceful as what happened outside today.'

'We were jus' stickin' up fer ourselves . . . Sir,' I stammered.

Dad-ak picked up a pencil and began to tap it on his desk. He stared at me as if I no longer deserved to exist as a human being.

My head lowered with a shame unknown.

As I stood shaking all over, listening to the tap-tap-tap of Dad-ak's pencil and the nervous squelching in my wet shoes, I shut my eyes and tried to fight back the tears by thinking of my beloved home town of Beckom.

But in my mind, all I could hear was the aching sound of wind through the silos, whistling my childhood goodbye.

Away in a Manger

After we'd finished collecting our clothing off the lawn we were taken to our dormitory. It was in McCaughey House, upstairs, nearest the toilets and showers.

'Best spot ta be,' Jug reckoned. 'Means we got a head start before the hot water runs out.'

The dorm itself was a large box-like room which smelt musty. It held a dozen kids, arranged bed – locker – bed – locker around the dorm, overflowing out onto the veranda. The thin grey metal lockers, which were to hold our belongings, stood in awkward balance. The floor covering was a blistered, patterned lino. The ceiling was dull, imprinted plaster, and the room had aged cream-coloured walls. Two tall windows faced out onto the veranda leading to the shower and toilet area.

'Joe use'ta be in this very same dorm,' Jug said with pride. ''E use'ta scoot through them windows when 'e got caught short. Ya not supposed ta though.'

The beds were made of chipped and rusted cream piping, loosely sprung. The lumpy mattresses were whitish with thin black flecks running down their length and filled with what Jug described as 'horse hair'. The old army issue blankets folded at the foot of the beds were grey with large reddish or blue stripes. Jug and I picked two spare beds beside each other.

When we'd changed into our khaki day clothing, Jug scrounged some string and tied it along the veranda.

'Knee-cessity is the mother'a invention,' he skited as we placed our muddied school uniforms on coat-hangers and hung them on the line. The others who'd been in the brawl followed suit.

A bell rang from over near the laundry. A stampeding sound echoed around us. Kids appeared from everywhere and started to thunder downstairs and out of McCaughey House as if a fire was raging through the dormitories.

'It's the dinner bell! Foller me!' Jug called as he joined in the charge.

By the time we reached the passage outside the dining room it was seething with kids of all shapes, sizes and ages, pushing and shoving into different queues. Jug and I tried to join a line.

'Piss off Grots. Down the back,' someone shouted.

After we'd found our First Year group a hand bell rang for us to enter. The Fifth Years filed in first, followed by the Fourth Years, Third, Second and lastly ourselves.

The vast dining room easily sat the two hundred or so students. Three rows of wooden tables, covered with red-and-white and blue-and-white chequered tablecloths, eating utensils, plates, bread and butter, stretched down its length. Three kids stood to attention at each side of the table with a Table Head at the top. The six of us who'd arrived that day were placed furthest from the kitchen area, which meant we were to be the last served. Our table head was a bloke called 'Hulk' Hansford; wiry, dark-skinned, shallow features, with an infectious laugh.

'Somethin' like a donkey shittin' bricks,' Jug later quipped.

The Nits (teachers), about ten in all, sat along the elevated front of the dining room, facing the students. The Duty Nit for the day was 'Ten Quid' Frobisher. Hulk explained that he'd been 'landed 'is moniker 'cause ten quid's how much it cost 'im ta immigrate from Pommie-land'.

When Ten Quid rang the bell we all fell silent. 'Our heavenly Father, we thank you for this food we eat. Amen.' The instant amen was spoken the dining room exploded into excited chatter. The noise of everyone being seated was deafening. Arms sprung out, diving for bread and butter.

From the kitchen area appeared the maids dressed in white. They pushed tray-mobiles up and down the aisles delivering steaming hot pots of tea, trays of cold lamb and bowls of salad. We passed the food down to Hulk who divided it into equal portions. I overheard a kid at the table behind me. 'Swap ya a slice'a meat fer a couple'a slices'a bread.' Everything seemed negotiable.

Ma Dad-ak, a stately, full-bodied woman, patrolled the aisles in her crisp Matron's uniform making sure that the operation ran smoothly. She barked orders at the maids and chastised kids for their lack of manners.

'Didn't your Mother ever teach you how to hold a knife and fork?' she roared at a kid a couple of tables away, making me double-check that I was holding my knife and fork like everyone else, just in case Mum had somehow got it wrong.

After we'd devoured our main course the kitchen maids took away our used plates then reappeared delivering stainless steel bowls of cold prunes and lumpy hot custard.

The end of dinner was signalled by the hand bell. When everyone had quietened, Ten Quid welcomed us six new arrivals. His words were greeted by muffled boos. Comments like, 'Who's missing Mummy,' shot through the air like barbed arrows.

When Ten Quid rang the bell again we stood to attention behind our chairs. Another ring dismissed us. The Fifth Years exited first, then the Fourth Years, Third, Second, then ourselves. It was apparent that we were to be last in line for everything.

After dinner we returned to our dorms to finish unpacking and make our beds.

'This is better'n Prep, eh?' Jug exclaimed, Prep being the nightly two hours of compulsory study.

As our washing was to be done in the school laundry, every item of clothing had to be marked with our names. While I was placing my clothes into my locker I had visions of Mum. All those late nights sitting hunched under dim light, her silver thimble, glasses hung low, sewing name tags onto shirt collars, socks, shorts and underpants. And when she'd run out of the tags that she'd had made up in Temora, she took to writing my name in indelible ink. I'd already begun to miss her.

'Come on mate. Buck up. Things'll be great, you'll see,' Jug said, sensing my longing.

Finally it was time for our nightly shower. In all, there were fifty of us First Years taking up the main upstairs dormitories in McCaughey House. Showering was a raucous, communal affair in a large, open-spaced chamber with white, tiled walls. Six showers stood on one side of the room in full view, a row of basins on the other, hooks on the side walls. Everyone waited in line for their turn.

I'd never stood naked in front of a group of strangers, and I could see that others were feeling awkward as well. A few even more so. While I had my towel wrapped tightly around me, I noticed how a couple of blokes wore their dressing gowns. At the last moment they hung their gowns on the wall hooks, washed themselves briskly with their backs turned, then scurried off to dry themselves.

There were also a few kids with overgrown foreskins. I'd never seen boys like that before. It looked weird, almost unnatural – 'Not circumnavigated', as Jug put it.

None of this nakedness seemed to worry Jug, not in the least. He paraded around without a care in the world.

'Look at that bloke's dick over there,' Jug said, digging me in the ribs. 'Blimey he's gonna cause some damage some day.'

Shyly, I turned away, suffering a flush of manly shame at how small mine was in comparison.

Jug struck up conversation with a bloke from our dorm, 'Bluey' Johnson. Bluey had already been at school for three days. He told us how a First Year kid had been given the strap the previous night by a Prefect for talking after lights out. And how he had been given the Royal Flush by some Second Years.

'They wanted ta bot some'a me chews. "Go and buy ya own," I says. That's when they dragged me off ta the dunny. Almost drowned me they did.'

Bluey was so distraught that he even wanted to take us down to the Mutch House toilets to show us the exact bowl he'd been dunked in. Jug shrugged it off as if it was an everyday occurrence.

'Seen one bowl, seen 'em all,' Jug said nonchalantly, then

called over the noise around us, 'See that shower there mate, well, that's the exact same one me brotha said a homesick bloke hanged himself on.'

Silence fell like a steamy fog. The bloke who was under the shower – the one with the large penis – scampered over to the row of basins to distance himself from the scene of the hanging.

'No bull,' Jug added. 'Me mate 'ere knows about it. Don't ya Swampy?'

All eyes turned to me. I nodded in agreement. With that, everyone stared up at the shower as if the body was still dangling there. But it didn't perturb Jug. He was into the deserted shower in a flash.

'Thanks "Meat",' he called out to the bloke still cringing by the basins, then merrily began to wash.

After our showers, we got ready for bed. Ten Quid arrived at the door and flicked the lights off and on. He explained that it was the sign for us to get into bed. 'Flicker', he called it. Flicker was followed by 'Lights Out'. No one was allowed to speak.

As darkness engulfed the dorm, thoughts of my parents flooded my mind. I'd been away from home without them twice before but, after the turmoil of the day, I longed to be tucked in and given my usual goodnight kiss. 'Sleep tight, Tiger mite', were the last words I heard before being overtaken by sleep.

But sleep refused to come that night.

I battled to make myself comfortable in my bed. The saggy mattress was like a hammock stuffed with cactus prickles. My every twitch and turn caused the bed springs to creak. The channel-bred mosquitoes buzzed relentlessly around my mozzie net.

The harder I struggled for sleep, the more the horror stories Jug had told us began to have a frightening ring of reality. As I lay listening for the sounds of home, the desperate urge come over me to find out if Jug had been fair dinkum about the homesick kid hanging himself in the showers.

Risking a strapping I leaned over. 'Jug! Jug!' I whispered.
But Jug was fast asleep.

My imagination then led me to the line of thinking that the real reason why my parents had sent me to Yanco Ag was to get me out of their hair. After soaking up their love like a human sponge, perhaps I'd exhausted them. They'd woken up one morning, looked at each other, and were struck with the same thought. 'Let's get rid of him. It's time we had a life to ourselves.'

I'd read of similar happenings in the Sydney *Daily Mirror*. Kids being sent to orphanages because their parents couldn't cope. It all started to make sense. That's why Mum had kept ringing the school, day after day, virtually pleading that I be given a placement.

Suddenly the eerie, foreign silence around me was broken by the voice of Bluey Johnson.

'Well, I'm not gonna get homesick,' he called out into the vacant night.

'Me neither,' came the reply.

Mister Swift and His Little Red PMG Van

Jug and I enter the tuck shop. Being First Years we've had to wait until everyone else has been served. We eye the display of lollies.

'Penny'a mixed, thanks Mr Blackwell,' Jug says.

'Same 'ere, thanks,' I say.

Our mouths water as the white paper bag is filled with chews.

'Thanks,' we both say.

On our way out, we pause at the tuckshop door. We look up and down the Mutch House lane checking for Second Years. The coast is clear. Jug and I scamper along the lane toward McCaughey House. Our destination is First Year Bush; acres of freedom. It's an unwritten law that no one but First Years can go out into First Year Bush.

'Hey youse Grots. Giss a chew.'

Jug and I freeze. We're ambushed. It's Rags, 'Moof' McTavish and 'Animal' Emery. They grab us by our shirt collars and drag us into the alcove of downstairs McCaughey House.

'Bugger off Rags,' Jug mumbles.

'Watcha say Ashton?'

'Nothin'.'

'Hey Rags. Them Grots forgot ta bow.'

Jug and I bob our heads in unison.

'Bow proper,' sneers Rags.

'Bugger off,' says Jug.

Both of us are held in a half nelson. We're pushed into the nearby toilet. I'm first. Animal clamps his thumb and fingers onto the back of my neck. My head is forced down the bowl. The porcelain is cold against my face. Jug's words of warning are pounding in my brain. 'Don't fight it. If ya kick up a stink, worse'll happen.'

The chain rattles. I hear the flush coming. It arrives in a mad swirl of water. Rags is laughing. The water gushes up my nose. I can't breathe. I start to cough and splutter. It stops. Animal releases his grip. I'm saturated. It's Jug's turn. He doesn't even flinch. Rags would love him to kick up a stink. Rags hates Jug.

'Okay youse Grots. Where's ya chews?'

We take the paper bags from our shorts pockets and hand them over. Rags grabs some chews for himself and his mates and gives us back what little remains.

'Bugger off Grots. Dob and ya dead.'

Jug and I scamper from the toilet, across the lawns and out into First Year Bush. We sit on a log and share what's left.

As we struggled within our new surroundings, Rags Kelly and his mates gave us hell. Yet it wasn't so much the bullying, but what it fuelled, that proved the most difficult to cope with.

Homesickness. That deep, hollow, loveless, feeling. Never before had I realised the importance of my family, my Mum in particular.

Those desperate longings were only given some relief when Mr Swift drove out from Yanco in his little red PMG van to deliver the weekly mail.

Thursday afternoon after school, those of us who weren't working on the school farm doing Stock Duty gathered out along the second storey McCaughey House veranda. All eyes were trained toward the school's front gate. The instant the dust from the PMG van rose above the red gums, my heart leapt into my throat. Along with my mates, I scampered down the double staircase and dashed down the road past Dad-ak's residence to greet Mr Swift. We cheered wildly as he flashed by with a smile as wide as Sydney Harbour Bridge arched over his face. We spun around in our tracks and chased him all the way back to the main entrance.

When Mr Swift jumped out of his van he was welcomed like a favourite Uncle. We slapped him on the back and bombarded him with questions.

'How's it goin' Mister Swift?'

'How's the Missus 'n kids?'

'Reckon it'll rain Mister Swift?'

Yet not for a single second did our eyes leave that large calico mail bag until it was safely on its way into the secretary's office.

Even when Mister Swift returned empty-handed we were still there, ready to send him on his way with a cheerio almost as enthusiastic as our welcome.

'See ya later Mister Swift,' we called, patting the back of the van as it drew away. 'Thanks for comin' . . . Thanks very much.'

After the van disappeared we remained outside McCaughey House, waving at that ever diminishing cloud of dust.

On the first mail day after we'd arrived at school I'd trailed Mr Swift into the office. I'd watched him pass the bag over the counter to Mr Harris, the secretary. I'd ogled at the mail being poured onto his desk.

'Couldn't have a quick look ta see if there's anythin' from me Mum, could ya Mister Harris?' I'd asked.

'You know the Head's orders,' he'd replied.

And I did.

Dad-ak had given strict instructions that First Years weren't to be sent any food packages, gifts, or extra pocket money. He wanted none of us to be better off than the rest. To ensure his orders were carried out, Mr Harris checked our mail.

So it wasn't until Thursday evening that we all gathered at the staff entrance of the dining room in readiness for the Duty Nit to hand out the mail. It felt like an eternity until my name was mentioned.

'Marsh!'

I elbowed my way through the pressing throng calling 'I'm right here Sir. It's for me. I'm comin' to get it,' just to make certain that the Duty Nit was aware of my presence. Then, with the letter safely in my hands, I rushed off to a secluded spot under a willow by the lake.

Just the mere sight of my Mother's handwriting was enough to bring the tears to my eyes. I hugged the letter to my heart for comfort. I smelt it, searching for reminders of home. The news it held seemed secondary. It was mostly about the daily happenings. I could picture it all so clearly. Anzac biscuits being baked in the kitchen oven. The pub on a Saturday night. A barbecue. A dust storm. The trials of harvest.

After reading the letter dozens of times over, I wandered back to my dorm. There we all handed our mail over to Bluey for him to read. Bluey rarely received mail. His Mum was the cook on a station somewhere between Hay and Booligal. She hadn't ever had the chance to learn how to read or write. But we knew that if she could, the sentiments would be the same.

On the occasions Mrs Johnson got one of the ringers to jot a note for her, we all helped Bluey try to decipher the page or so. More often than not, those letters seemed as if they'd been written with a thumbnail dipped in tar.

We were in such a buoyant mood after we received mail. We sat around our dorm telling wild stories about our families; our old home life; the way things used to be. And then we imagined what would happen if our mothers smuggled themselves out to school in the back of Mr Swift's little red PMG van.

'The first thing my Mum'd do 'd be ta grab Rags 'n 'is mates 'n cut 'em down ta size. Give 'em a good swift kick in the duds 'n a clip over the lug-hole,' Meat boasted.

' 'N they'd bawl their eyes out like the little babies they are,' Bluey added, ' 'n we wouldn't give two hoots, eh?!'

Howling Chorus

Jug reckoned that, from the day Yanco Ag opened, the students had to pitch in and help out on the school farm. And that's why, by the time we arrived, 'Stock Duty', as we called it, had become such an important part of school life. For two weeks out of six, everyone, except the Fifth Years, was rostered onto helping out in the dairy, piggery, poultry, in the 'vegie' gardens, school gardens, and for sporting events.

The first Stock Duty I was ever rostered on was Sports Stock.

We didn't have a pool at school. So when it was our turn to host the Riverina High School's Swimming Championships, we used Leeton Memorial Swimming Pool. Each morning and afternoon Bluey and I, plus two Second Years, two Third Years and a Fourth Year Stock Leader reported to the front of McCaughey House. There, Dad-ak loaded us into the wire cage on the back of the school's Bedford truck, drove us into Leeton and supervised our work, before bringing us back to school.

Bluey and I were a miserable sight, with both of us battling through the worst of the homesickness. We hunched up together in the corner of the truck to shield ourselves from the whipping wind while the Second Years chided us.

'Who's a little homesick baby.'

'Little sookie babes.'

None of that helped us much; nor did working in the strict company of Dad-ak.

'A man's only as good as the sum total of his labours,' he bellowed one morning after I'd laid down my spanner to tie a boot lace.

'But my shoe laces have come undone.'

'Then you should be wearing gum boots on this job, son.'
'Yes sir,' I said, and went back to work.

I doubted if anyone ever won an argument with Dad-ak.

Around the same time, Bluey must have written to his Mum telling her about how homesick he was. Mrs Johnson lived for her son. She was a widow; her husband had died in a rodeo accident.

After receiving Bluey's letter, Mrs Johnson decided to borrow the station ute and drive over from Hay to cheer him up. She arrived at school on the Saturday afternoon only to be told that her son was working at Leeton pool. When she got to the pool we were busy setting up the stands. The instant Bluey saw his Mum, he dropped his end of the scaffold and shot off to greet her.

When Dad-ak saw what was going on, all hell broke loose. He stormed over and ordered Bluey back on the job. Mrs Johnson was stunned speechless. Then as Bluey reluctantly dragged himself back to the stands, Dad-ak ushered her around the side of the dressing shed. They were almost out of ear shot but we could still hear them going hammer and tongs.

Somewhere along the line Mrs Johnson shouted 'Well, whose bloody son is 'e anyway!'

Dad-ak came back with 'That's irrelevant! If they've got a job to do then, they *must* do it.'

When Dad-ak returned he ordered us, Bluey included, to get back onto the truck and said we'd return on Sunday morning to complete the stands. As we were about to leave, Mrs Johnson appeared from out of the toilets with a hankie covering her face. When we took off, she followed. Before long she was driving close enough behind for us to see that she was crying.

Bluey snapped. He started to clamber over the top of the wire cage. I was scared that he'd jump. While our Stock Leader tried to drag him back into the truck, I started banging on the roof of the driver's cab to get Dad-ak to stop.

To this day I don't know whether Dad-ak heard me or not.

But no matter how much noise I made, he remained hunched over the steering wheel, glaring down the length of the Leeton to Yanco road with his foot planted firmly on the accelerator.

Through Yanco township we went with Bluey yelling out from the back of the truck to his Mum. The people we passed must have thought that he was being kidnapped.

In the end I gave up trying to get Dad-ak's attention and went to comfort Bluey. 'We'll be back at school soon mate. Everythin'll be okay.'

Then I made a fatal mistake.

I started looking at Mrs Johnson. And the more I looked at her, the more she started to look like my own Mum. And the more Bluey's Mum started to look like my own Mum, the more I began to imagine that she *was* my own Mum.

Before I knew it, there I was, crying right along with Bluey.

Sporadic snorts and sobs broke out behind me. I turned around and, to my surprise, the big, brave Second Years had begun bawling. Once they'd got going, they in turn kick-started the Third Years. Eventually it was even too much for our Fourth Year Stock Leader. He dropped his bundle and burst into tears.

By the time we reached the school gates, the whole seven of us were clinging to the wire cage howling our eyes out at Mrs Johnson, who was howling her eyes out back at us.

But no amount of tears were going to get Dad-ak to stop. He continued up the drive as if nothing was happening. Even when we arrived at McCaughey House, Mrs Johnson wasn't allowed to see Bluey. Us boys were sent off to clean the sports shed and she was told that she had to wait until he'd finished Stock Duty.

'Five o'clock and not a moment sooner.'

She sat and waited.

The Portrait

A ghost lives in McCaughey House. One night, some kids saw it stalking through their dorm. They described it as being 'a hazy sorta white; thicker 'n a cloud, but human like'.

'Gawd almighty. Do ya reckon it was for real?' asked Meat.

'You bet it's for real,' Jug replied. 'Why, when me brotha was at Yanco Ag, he was havin' a quiet puff in the dunny one night 'n the ghost floated right past the door.'

'Gawd almighty,' Meat gasped.

'Joe reckons 'e shot out'a that bog, whiter 'n the ghost 'imself.'

'Gawd almighty. 'E would'a.'

'Joe swears it were the ghost'a Sir Samuel McCaughey.'

'Gawd almighty. Ya' kiddin'.'

'Jus' ask "Dozy", 'e knows all about the ghost.'

Dozy Dobkins was our Dorm Prefect. Jug reckoned he'd got his nickname after he fell asleep in the luggage rack of a train on his way home to Junee one holidays and didn't wake up until Central Railway Station, twelve hours later. But other than being able sleep like a log, Dozy was also touted as a bit of a ghost historian, and he backed up Joe's claim.

'There've been thirty clear sightin's of the ghost,' Dozy told us, 'and, in every case, it had a strikin' resemblance to that of Sir Samuel McCaughey in his portrait hangin' outside Dad-ak's office down near the front entrance.'

'Gawd almighty,' exclaimed Meat.

Dozy went on to say that the first reported sighting was three years to the day after Sir Samuel McCaughey had died, back in 1922, the year Yanco Ag opened as a school.

'One of the domestic staff, a hard-workin' but quiet girl nicknamed "Mona Lisa" was readin' a romantic novel in bed one hot, still, summer's night with the moon lookin' like a bright, golden penny. The book was reachin' its climax when out of nowhere an icy breeze swept in through her open window. When she looked up, there it was, the ghost, wrapped in a foggy swirl, standin' right at the foot of her bed.

'To her terror, the foggy swirl began to move toward her. Inch by inch it spun itself up along the side of her bed. When it was near the bedhead, a hand reached out from the foggy swirl and ever so slowly it started to pull back the sheet that she was cowerin' under.

'Mona attempted to scream. But, bein' in such a panic-stricken state, her throat seized up. Nothin' came out but a long low moanin' sound. A sound like a young heifer when she's mated first up.

'When Mona didn't turn up for work the followin' mornin', Mrs Breakwell, the Headmaster's wife, went lookin' for her. She found the girl in her bed. Thankfully she was still alive, though it was obvious that she'd suffered a great trauma. Mona's eyes had a glazed look about them. The book she was readin' had been thrown out the window. Her sheets were torn to shreds. Her night-dress was missin'. She lay there as naked as the day she was born, a thin wisp of a smile etched on her lips.

'"He sort'a looked a bit like the chap in that picture outside Mister Breakwell's office," Mona reportedly told the staff.

'The picture – or paintin' as it was – Mona mentioned, was none other than the portrait of Sir Samuel McCaughey. Yet, though she seemed very definite about it being a male ghost with a strong likeness to Sir Samuel, Mona seemed reluctant about going into any further detail. After all, the ghost was wrapped in a thick foggy swirl.'

'Gawd almighty.'

Dozy reckoned that the experience pushed Mona over the edge and she never recovered from the ordeal. Her youthful innocence had vanished. Whenever she looked at the portrait, a strange tingling sensation spread over her body, followed by hot flushes. Then she became touched by a type of madness.

She sat in front of the portrait day in, day out, suffering through her attacks like she was punishing herself. Her work went by the wayside.

Mrs Breakwell eventually had to dismiss her.

A couple of days after Dozy told us the story about Mona Lisa, Meat was waiting outside Dad-ak's office after being caught smoking. While he was building himself up for a caning, he was struck by the feeling that someone was staring at him. When he turned around, the eyes in the portrait of Sir Samuel McCaughey had fixed on him in a eerie, piercing, icy glare. If he moved to the left of the portrait, the eyes followed him. If he moved to the right, the eyes moved with him. But before Meat had the chance to carry out a closer investigation, Dad-ak had latched onto his ear and was dragging him into the office. After his caning, the portrait completely slipped his mind. But later that night, Meat woke up, plagued by nagging thoughts. Was what he'd heard and seen over the past few days for real or not? And if it was, could the ghost of McCaughey possibly *live* in the portrait?

Normally Meat was one of the most placid and docile of kids. Jug reckoned the only thing that'd get him moving was if someone stuck a stick of dynamite under him. But on that still summer's night, with the moon looking like a bright, golden penny, curiosity overtook Meat and it wouldn't let him go back to sleep.

Eventually it all got too much. The questions running around in his brain just had to be answered. Meat got out of bed, grabbed a box of matches and tip-toed out of the dorm.

Even though the night was hot, the lino floor felt cold on Meat's bare feet. At the top of the double staircase he was almost scared off by the moonlight shining through the giant lead-light design of the shepherdess tending sheep.

Step by step, down the staircase he went. Occasionally there'd be a creak. He'd stop to let the noise die down before going on. There were Duty Nits about and Meat was only too well aware of the strife he'd be in if he was caught wandering around in the dead of the night. Finally he reached the bottom of the staircase. He walked easier along the carpet that led to the main entrance.

At the portrait Meat paused to make doubly sure that no one was about. When he was satisfied that the coast was clear, he took a match from the box and lit it. Even though he was tall for his age, he still had to hold the lit match as high as possible to get a closer look.

Meat was standing there, stretched to his limit, gazing into Sir Samuel McCaughey's eyes, when an icy breeze swept down the length of the corridor. Meat felt a strange presence, the like he'd never known. The flame of the match fluttered, then blew out. As he stood terrified in the darkness, a hand pressed down on his shoulder.

'What are you doing, son?'

Meat let out such a hell of a scream that it even woke Dozy. He took off so fast that Jug reckons he could make out the scorch marks down the length of the carpet.

It wasn't until three o'clock in the morning that we found Meat over in the class block, quaking under his desk. As much as we tried to convince him that it'd only been the Duty Nit, 'Legs' Blackwell, who'd crept up behind him, he wouldn't believe us.

Right up until the day he was to leave school, Meat broke out into uncontrollable shakes whenever he had to wait outside Dad-ak's office, under the fixing stare of Sir Samuel McCaughey.

'Ranting' O'Reilly

If ever we were in need of a good argument, Tuesdays after school in Room 2B was the place to go. That's where the debating group met and they'd argue the toss about anything.

It didn't matter what anybody said during the course of a school day, no one took the slightest notice. But as soon as you took one step inside Room 2B and opened your gob, you'd be told that whatever you'd just said was dead wrong.

Bluey once got caught in a downpour while he was walking across the quadrangle. Inadvertently he headed toward Room 2B to take cover. When he burst through the door, wringing wet, he announced, 'It's raining cats and dogs out there.' And immediately five blokes wanted to take up issue that it wasn't.

The leader of the debating group was 'Ranting' O'Reilly.

Ranting came from a family of devout 'Tykes', as Jug called Catholics, who hailed from Collingullie. His Dad was a share-farmer. And, with fifteen kids – eight boys and seven girls – Jug reckoned that his Mum wouldn't have been sure who she was half the time. Still, with a mob like that, there wasn't only a lot to talk about, there was also a lot to talk about it with. Ranting's first challenge in life was how to get heard. He managed well. By the time he was ten he had a voice like a foghorn and could talk the leg off a table.

But on arrival at Yanco Ag, he found that he couldn't get a decent bite out of anyone. If he contradicted anything the more senior students said, they'd give him a clip under the ear. The kids in his own year soon cottoned on that Ranting had a strong opinion on just about everything, and if he didn't, he'd make one up. So as soon as he opened his mouth, they'd simply ignore him.

At the end of his tether, Ranting approached 'Thomp'

Thornton, the English Master, with the idea of forming a debating group, as he'd heard happened in other schools around the area.

The response to the advertisement they placed on the school's noticeboard was slow. Being a male-only agricultural boarding school, the major topics of the day usually revolved around sport, sex and the weather. The idea of getting stuck into something like 'The positive and negative ramifications of the Industrial Revolution on Australian society' was too mind-boggling.

But Ranting, along with Thomp, stuck with it, and gradually they gathered together a small band of students.

'Kids,' as Jug put it, 'who liked airin' their lungs about anythin' from the politics'a the day, to how many tits there was on a bull.'

Even so, after a year of four blokes arguing against each other, it got to the stage where all concerned knew what the others were about to say even before they said it. Things started to get stale and comments like, 'You can't get a decent argument anywhere around here,' didn't raise a hackle. New challenges were needed, along with fresh ideas and topics. That's when it was decided to launch the Yanco Agricultural High School Debating Group into the hurly-burly of inter-school competition.

There was one particular subject that Ranting couldn't handle. Coming from such a strict family of Tykes, if anyone uttered a single word against the Pope the fluff on the back of his neck stood up like barbed wire. He'd clench his fists until his knuckles went white. He'd tremble with rage so much that his ears would vibrate. Then he'd completely lose control.

And that's exactly what happened during the group's inaugural outing at the Inter-School Debating Championships.

Ranting and his mob had taken all before them until they reached the finals against Griffith High School. The subject was: 'Whether or not the reparation payments imposed on Germany after World War I were a direct cause of Adolf Hitler gaining power.'

Yanco Ag looked like winning hands down until Griffith's last speaker took the floor. The bloke stood for a moment absorbing the atmosphere. He looked this way and that at the expectant audience. He gave a smirk to his mates. Then he looked Ranting square in the eye and shouted, 'THE POPE STINKS!'

Obviously the bloke had been given the tip about Ranting's personal feelings. But just in case Ranting hadn't heard clearly the first time, the bloke repeated it again, only a little louder: 'THE POPE *STINKS!!*'

Just who'd let the cat out of the bag no one ever discovered.

They didn't have the chance.

Before the bloke could open his trap again, Ranting leapt over the table and a scuffle of gigantic proportions broke out.

Due to that unfortunate fracas, Yanco Ag were, in effect, banned from taking part in further inter-school debating forums.

After the group returned to school and the news spread about the stoush, quite a few of us kids started thinking that there might be more fun to this debating caper than we'd first imagined. Within a week, Ranting had massed enough devoted supporters to whip up a verbal storm. There was only one basic rule. Out of due respect, it was preferred that little mention be made of religion and definitely none be made of the Pope.

Although the debating group remained starved for outside opposition, it gained enough momentum out of the incident to carry on after Ranting left school and became a Labor backbencher in the New South Wales Parliament.

In the Swim

Jug reckons that, just three weeks after Yanco Ag opened, a kid drowned.

'Frank Sherman was 'is name. The poor bugger hadn't even been at school long enough to've landed a nickname,' Jug says, moved by the mishap.

Apparently, because the parts for the water pump to McCaughey House hadn't arrived, the students used the river for their needs. It was during a mass wash-in that Frank disappeared.

'For a while there they thought that maybe a bunyip or somethin' might'a snatched 'im,' Jug continues. 'But, it hadn't. A couple'a weeks later they fished 'is body out'a the river. There weren't a bunyip scratch on 'im.'

It was then that Ernest Breakwell, the Headmaster, decided to hold an annual Beach Carnival. His idea was that getting the students to compete against each another would spur them on to learn how to swim. And so from such tragic beginnings the Beach Carnival grew to become the first major sporting event on our school calendar.

'No one's drowned since.'

As soon as the fresh intake of First Years arrive, preparations begin. After tea on the first Wednesday the new students are ordered to gather on the quadrangle with a white singlet in hand, clearly marked with their name. There they are to be organised into their House groups.

It's a confusing process as to which kid goes into what House. To the untrained eye it might look like an Arab sheep market, with kids being pushed, pulled and shoved in all directions.

The First Years aren't given any say as to which House they want to join. If someone in their family has previously attended

Yanco Ag, they automatically join the House the relative had belonged to. That's how Jug ended up in McCaughey House, because of Joe. Someone who is reasonably sports-like is keenly sought after by the House Captain and his Fifth Year cohorts. That's how I ended up in Gardiner House. The 'dregs', the studious and puny types, are worthless. Scholastic brilliance doesn't make for heaps of house points. They're the last selected.

After an hour or so of wrangling and haggling, the First Years find themselves divided into four groups, and their singlets are collected for dying. Green is for Gardiner, yellow for Breakwell, reddish/maroon, depending on the state of the dye, for McCaughey, and those who are in Mutch House don't have their singlets dyed because their colour is white.

For the next week everyone gathers in their House groups outside the dining room after tea, before heading in opposite directions out into the school's bush for marching practice. The House Captain and his mates keep a deadly eye on the new-comers. They are screamed at and ordered about, and if they get out of step, they are given a few sharp whacks around the legs with a gum sapling.

As time is short, those who can't swim are given lessons. The favoured method is sink-or-swim. That's where the non-swimmer is picked up and hurled into the river. Oddly enough, in most cases, the fear of drowning is enough to make the non-swimmer able to scramble to the safety of the bank in a manic thrashing of arms, legs and gasps for breath.

By the day of the Beach Carnival most kids can swim and march and, more importantly, are fired with the belief that the opposition is the most despicable scum on earth.

Many are the times that competitive spirits get out of hand and mateships are forgotten or ill-feelings revenged. So much so that a couple of Nits have to be stationed in Dad-ak's tin boat, near the basketball rounding buoy. Their job is to fish out the kids who have been dragged under, mauled or knocked senseless as we fight tooth and nail, not only for precious

House points, but also for the honour to represent our school at the Riverina Swimming Championships.

Once the day is over, friendships return to normal and ill feelings are exhausted. Most are anyway. We sit around together and talk wildly of how Yanco Ag could thrash any school in the Riverina if they dared take us on at a beach carnival.

But they never do.

The Inter-School Swimming Carnival is always held in the clear, still waters of an olympic pool. And having had the river as our only swimming venue, that's where we run into a couple of major problems.

Firstly, the river is so muddy that we learn to swim with our heads in the air like periscopes, which gives us some hope of seeing where we were going. This swimming style is known as 'the Murrumbidgee Muddle'. Secondly, because of the river current, we navigate in a wide arc out and around the anchored basketball, so we find it difficult to swim in a straight line, especially when we're stuck in a pool between lane ropes.

As Jug and I enter our second year we've got a fair idea how to march and swim, and certainly how to stir each other up.

'Youse blokes in Gardiner are gonna get the pants whipped off'a ya,' Jug chides me, priming himself for the contest.

'You and whose army?' I bite back.

'Jus' you wait,' says he.

'I'll be waitin',' says me.

'Swamp fox,' he hisses.

'Big ears,' I sneer.

We both fall silent; me imagining that I'd just beaten Jug by a whisker in the beach sprint, and him probably imagining the same thing, except with the placings reversed.

Then we go back to the serious business at hand.

'What odds ya reckon we should offer on Troy's Boy in the fifth at Randwick?'

On the morning of the Beach Carnival, not only the temperature is near boiling point – so are the tempers. Rags Kelly and Crash Cameron have been niggling each other all the way down the track to School Beach. When Rags says a few things about Crash's Mum, it gets serious. A bit of push and shove breaks out between the two. Crash throws a haymaker. Rags, who is ready for a fight most times of the day or night, retaliates. Before you can say Jack Robinson, they're at it, hammer and tongs.

A tight circle forms around the two as they roll about in the dust. The chant of 'Fight! Fight!' starts up. It's interrupted by a car horn. It's Dad-ak and Ma Dad-ak driving down to the Carnival in the school ute. The circle peels away leaving the two wrestling on the ground.

'In my office after dinner,' Dad-ak barks as he drives slowly by.

Rags and Crash jump to their feet and return to their House groups, snarling at each other. I wonder what'll happen when they meet in the water.

Stoked by the heat and the fight, the tension on the bank above the beach is electric. Green singlets seethe at red, yellow at white as we prepare for the March Past. When Dad-ak and Ma Dad-ak are settled, the all-clear is given for the Beach Carnival to begin.

'QUICK MARCH!'

The first group, McCaughey House, lurches into action. I get a glance of Jug amongst the blur of red. Determination is etched on his face. Down the bank his group sweep in a flail of arms, legs and stamping feet. The instant they hit the sand, everything changes. They sprout wings. They start squawking like a pack of startled galahs and fly across the beach to land with an almighty splash in the cool of the river. Jug is somewhere in the middle of them.

In the confusion of the moment it doesn't quite register on us in Gardiner House what the actual problem might be. Perhaps we're just so fired up with how much tougher we are than the McCaughey House scumbags that no one even gives a thought that the sand might being scalding hot. Our House Captain yells, 'QUICK MARCH!' and I, along with the rest, throw back my chin, stick out my chest and plough into the molten sand.

In a flash we've joined McCaughey House in the river.

Like two packs of dim-witted lemmings, Breakwell then Mutch House follow suit. Before we know it, there we all are – McCaughey, Gardiner, Breakwell and Mutch – riveted in the river, gazing up at Dad-ak as if we're there for a mass baptism.

While we're standing around in the water wondering how to get back across the beach into the shade, I spy Jug.

'I'm still waitin',' I call.

'Swamp fox,' he retorts.

'Big ears,' I shout back.

We both laugh.

Eventually Dad-ak decides the sand should be ploughed over. That in itself turns out to be a debacle. When 'Ape' finally gets back with the International, he bogs it. Then someone goes and gets the Farmall. By the time all the bogging, unbogging, changing over of the plough and the ploughing of the beach is completed, most of us are suffering from heat stroke as well as blistered, burnt feet.

Dad-ak calls off the Beach Carnival.

A week later at Leeton Memorial Swimming Pool our non-existent preparations are soon reflected in the results. Our normally intimidating school war cry is reduced to a whimper as our sunburnt swimmers bob awkwardly up and down the pool, battling gallantly against the lane ropes.

Of all our less-than-impressive results at the Riverina Schools Swimming Championship, this is our second poorest on record.

The worst was in 1956. That year the Beach Carnival was cancelled because no one could get within cooee of the beach.

It was twenty foot under water.

Paradise Lost

It was the most fleeting of glances. I was standing beside the running track with my mates when she flashed by like a thoroughbred mare on her way to win the Riverina Senior Schoolgirls 110 yard sprint.

She wouldn't have even seen me. And at the time, I remember thinking that she was old enough to be my sister. But there was a certain something else about her; something that I couldn't quite describe.

Later that day 'Tubby' Tisato, from Saint Francis College, and I were locked in a do-or-die contest to avoid running last in the thirteen-years-and-under boys mile. In my delirious state the strangest of things happened. As Tubby and I staggered down the straight, matching stride for stride, she returned to me as a vision of splendid, naked beauty.

It was the first time that I'd experienced a blinding physical attraction for a girl and it caused stirrings in parts of my body where there'd never been stirrings. By the time I got back into stride, Tubby had cruised ahead like a Cadillac. I was left gasping in his wake to collapse over the finishing line in humiliating last place.

Then, amid the mayhem of nausea, dizziness and my mates trying to get me breathing and walking again, she was forgotten. I returned to school and slipped back into the daily routine as if nothing had happened; bar of course, a last placing in the thirteen-years-and-under boys mile.

So what made her turn up a month or so later on that lonely beach in paradise was beyond me.

There I was, lying on the silver sands with a coral lagoon lapping at my feet, the warm air comforting my body like a woollen blanket. Behind me stretched a lush tropical mountain landscape leading up to a simmering volcano. The sky was postcard blue. I happened to roll over and saw her, away in the distance. She was instantly recognisable because of the way she ran with her black hair flowing behind her like a mane and her arms and legs working in perfect synchronisation.

It puzzled me for a moment why I couldn't pick the maroon colour of her Narrandera High School sports uniform. Then as she came nearer I began to make out the fine lines of her glistening naked body, her small jiggling breasts and the furry bit between her legs. It was then that those odd stirrings I'd experienced at the sport's carnival returned with a vengeance.

The smell of ash from the volcano started to fill the air. My heart began to beat with the sound of tom-toms. Soon, she was standing beside me. And all those years of accumulated snippets of womanly nonsense were suddenly whipped up into a whirl of emotion.

She knelt down and began kissing me. I returned her kisses with terrifying passion. A thousand-piece orchestra sprang up out of the tropical jungle and began playing. Fire crackers ignited in my head. The tom-toms beat louder. The volcano vibrated deep in the bowels of the earth.

We became entangled. Skin against skin. Flesh against flesh. The orchestra ripped into a wild frenzy. The tom-toms went crazy. The rumbles from the volcano shook the earth.

There was no peace from this madness. Yet more than anything, I wanted to go to the limit and beyond. I wanted to reach out to eternity.

So did she.

It was all too much for that little Island Paradise. Something eventually had to give.

And it did. It was the volcano.

Up it went in one almighty eruption that racked my body to the very core of its soul and left me quivering under a mass of hot, sticky lava.

I'd only heard it spoken about in secret; about wet dreams. But I hadn't taken much notice. It was like a newspaper headline, 'Cricket ball kills spectator.' Millions of people would read a line like that and laugh at the impossible odds of the same thing happening to them. The same with a wet dream. I never imagined it happening to me.

As I was trying to piece my dismal chain of events together, the memorable barrage the Catholic kids got from their Priest came to mind. Father Beltrame had sent massive shock waves through the school when, during one of his fire and brimstone sermons, he announced that harbouring dirty thoughts was a mortal sin.

I froze with the image of God shaking his head in total disgust. I began to plead my innocence. 'It was an accident God. It had nothing to do with me; things just got out of control during a dream. Dreams aren't for real.'

But I got the feeling that God wasn't convinced, and a bunch of angels were called over to help sit in judgement.

'Hey,' God said to the angels. 'Just 'ave a listen to this dork. What do you reckon. Is he tryin' to pull the wool over my eyes or not?'

So I struck a momentous deal; one which was to change my existence upon this earth. I vowed to God that I'd never have a dirty thought, ever again, in my entire life. Plus that when I left school I'd become a Christian missionary in the deep, dark depths of Africa, where I'd carry out the Lord's work until my dying day.

Only then, after I'd made that solemn oath, did I feel that God had a change of heart, and I was placed on probation.

But I wasn't out of the woods just yet. There was a more immediate and practical problem to be solved. Namely, how was I going to hide my stained sheets and pyjamas from the ladies who worked in the laundry? Nothing got past the laundry ladies. They were like a pack of gossiping parrots. Once they'd discovered a glob of dried tomato sauce on the fly of the pants I'd worn to the school dance. There was hell to pay over that. When the news reached Dad-ak, he'd dragged me into his office and called me 'the lowest of filthy animals'.

'If I had a daughter,' Dad-ak had rained down upon me, 'you'd be the last bloke on this earth I'd allow her to keep company with.'

If I could get into that much trouble over a bit of tomato sauce, what would happen here? After the laundry ladies found out, the news would spread like wildfire. I'd become the laughing stock of the entire school. I'd be known as the bloke who went barmy in the night and wet his bed over girls. Nobody would want a friend with a reputation like that. And I couldn't blame them. I'd become an outcast, like 'Wombat' Watson after he got caught with the teat suction cups down at the milking bails.

But the most soul-destroying thing was that I felt I'd never be able to trust myself again. I'd never be me, the person of the past. The one I knew so well before the running of the Riverina Senior Schoolgirls 110 yard sprint. The one who Jug virtually demanded should become his second-in-command because I was the most trustworthy and reliable bloke in our gang.

As I lay there struggling to come to grips with the mountain of forces that had landed me in such a mess, the penny suddenly dropped.

'I'm a man,' I said to myself. 'I'm a man.'

Then I burst into tears.

Einstein

'Back in my day we 'ad a bloke, Eric Erickson,' Jug's brother Joe began. '"Einstein", we called 'im, 'cause 'e idolised Albert Einstein the scientist. Well, this 'ere Einstein bloke didn't fit in around the place. 'E didn't play sport. Real puny 'e was. So 'e was the bloke at the end'a the peckin' order. The kid everyone got stuck inta.

'Well, not long after we arrived, Einstein got on the wrong end'a a couple'a hidin's. I tell ya Swamp, if he weren't weird before, 'e certainly was after. 'Is faraway gawk, gawked farther away. 'E got a nervous twitch. 'E started yabberin' to 'imself. Then 'e started disappearin' from our dorm at night 'n not returnin' 'til the early hours'a the mornin'.

'"Hey, Einstein," I says to 'im, "whatcha up ta?"

'"Freedom," 'e whispers, 'n wouldn't say no more.

'Then one evenin' jus' before tea some kids saw Einstein sittin' on top'a the roof'a McCaughey House. A beat-up ol' canvas bag, holdin' 'is belongin's, was strapped to 'is back. On 'is head 'e wore 'n ol' leather World War I flyin' cap 'n goggles. Beside him was a set'a wings made from balsa wood 'n newspaper with chook's feathers glued all over 'em.

'The whole school gathered below. While the Nits was workin' out how ta get 'im down, a group'a kids began yellin', "JUMP!"

'"Einstein's flipped his lid," someone shouts.

'But Einstein was a blank to the racket goin' on below. 'E started makin' 'is pre-flight checks. 'E radioed an imaginary flight control tower ta see if the runway was clear. He checked the weather cock ta get wind direction. He gawked at a map 'n took a compass bearing. 'E slipped 'is arms inta 'is wings, gave a couple'a warm-up flaps. One! . . . Two! . . . Then, with an almighty push, 'e slid down the roof 'n took off inta the sky.

'It were lucky that the hedge was where it is today Swamp, right across the lane from the laundry, 'cause when Einstein crash-landed a split second after take off, that hedge was the only thing that saved 'im from anythin' worse 'n a broke arm, bruises 'n abrasions.

'But Swamp, I saw somethin' in Einstein that day, somethin' that no one else saw; call it me sixth sense if ya like. So I decides ta go 'n see Einstein in sick bay. And that's where 'e promised ta provide me with information so as I'd make me fortune. 'N in return, I promised ta help 'im escape from school.

'By the time 'e got out'a sick bay, Einstein 'ad designed a special sort'a car that they use'ta use durin' World War I. "Freedom II", 'e named it.

'Ta me, "Freedom II" looked nothin' more 'n a forty-four gallon drum on wheels, which it was really. But Einstein reckoned that hidden inside that drum was the mechanics'a turnin' a 4:2:1 ratio of pig, cow 'n horse shit inta raw explosive engine power.

'I tell ya Swamp, it were a hell-of-a job buildin' that car. While 'e worked on the technical side'a things, I scrounged, borrowed 'n pinched pipin', wheels, drums, axles 'n whatever other odds 'n sods 'e needed. Then, aft'a most'a the term, "Freedom II" was ready 'n we set about blendin' up the 4:2:1 fuel mix.

'When all was okydoky, Einstein strapped 'is beat up ol' canvas bag, with 'is belongin's, onta 'is back. 'E put on 'is ol' leather World War I flyin' cap 'n goggles; checked wind direction, gawked at a map, took a compass bearin' and called, "Fire it up Joe!"

'But, we must'a somehow got the fuel ratio wrong, 'cause no sooner 'ad I fired it up than it exploded in a shower'a shit, metal, rubber, piping and odds and sods. I tell ya Swamp, it were a real mess.

'Then, while Einstein was in sick bay recoverin' from 'is injuries 'e designed a sailin' raft named "Freedom III". Perhaps after havin' failed to escape by air 'n land, 'e thought 'e'd 'ave a go at water.

'As soon as 'e was let out'a sick bay, we got stuck inta buildin' the sailin' raft. We strapped dead redgum logs together with rope. We stuck empty ten gallon drums along the sides so it'd float. Across the top we made a cabin outa half 'n ol' rainwater tank; ran a mast up through the tank ta hold the sheet we knocked off from the laundry, which was actin' as sails.

'Then one day I ran across Einstein down by the river about ta set sail. The Murrumbidgee was runnin' a right banker.

'"Surely," I says, "being picked on ain't 'arf as bad as bein' drowned."

'But, Einstein wouldn't 'ave a bar of it.

'"That's not the point, Joe," he says, strappin' the ol' beat up canvas bag to his back. He put on his World War I flyin' cap 'n goggles, checked wind direction, gawked at 'is map, took a compass bearin' 'n launched himself out inta the river.

''N Swamp, as those swirlin' waters started whippin' 'im away, 'e calls back. "Hey Joe," 'e says, "why don't ya run a book on this one? You'll make ya fortune if I get ta the weir," which, jus' between you'n me Swamp, I did.

''N ya know what? Three days later Einstein become the first person ta raft over Gogeldrie Weir, 'n survive.'

Miracle Man

For six days out of seven 'Wiz' Watson's Dad was a wheat cocky at Barmedman. On the seventh, Sunday, he'd strip off his dungarees, scrub up a bit, slip into a pair of black pants, put a white-collared shirt on back to front and head off to preach at his local church.

Wiz once told us that his Dad hadn't always been religious. The transformation had only occurred after Mrs Watson eloped with the travelling Rawleigh's man. Apparently the bloke had arrived one spring morning laden with a car full of ointments and potions, ready to cure all sorts of ailments from ingrown toe nails to brewer's droop. Then something happened over their first cup of tea. Something clicked. A violent passion erupted. By mid-afternoon when the Rawleigh's man drove back out the farm gate, Mrs Watson was packed in beside him.

When Wiz and his Dad returned from the sheep sales, the house was empty. All they could find was a scattered box of ointments and a business card which read:

RAWLEIGH'S PRODUCTS
SATISFACTION GUARANTEED

It was like the carpet had been ripped out from under them. At first Mr Watson tried to seek refuge in the bottle. Then one night, when he'd hit rock bottom, God made a special trip down to earth to have a heart-to-heart chat. It was during their deep discussion that God announced to Mr Watson that he'd been chosen to carry on the Lord's work in the church at Barmedman.

Mr Watson politely explained that there wasn't a church within cooee of Barmedman; never had been. The nearest was over at West Wyalong, a good twenty or thirty miles away. But God countered by telling him not to worry about that because Mr Watson, himself, was soon to build the church, and it'd be named the 'Holy Waters Church' after the local mineral springs.

Still and all, Wiz's Dad wasn't convinced that he was the right bloke for the job. Barmedman was a pretty wild town in those days. He wasn't much with the hammer and nails. It all seemed like a lot of hard yakka for nil return. That was until he asked God the age-old question, 'Well, what's in it for me?'

God replied that, in exchange for his heavenly labours, he'd be given supernatural powers; powers that'd enable him to perform miracles. As a demonstration God instructed Mr Watson to walk out onto the veranda and cast his hand over the maturing wheat crop. And lo and behold, what looked like a ten bag per acre crop was harvested three weeks later at a bumper eighteen bags per acre. It was enough to make the man swear off the drink. With the extra money from the harvest, Mr Watson ordered a huge truck-load of lumber and started to build the Holy Waters Church, a block back from the main street, where it still stands today – just.

After hearing Wiz tell his Dad's story, Jug piped up and said, 'Well Wiz, I reckon the only way a ten bag crop could turn inta eighteen bags would'a been fer ya old man to've used a very liberal amount'a bullshit.' Which, in truth, most of us thought he probably had. But the joke didn't get through to Wiz. He idolised his Dad.

Wiz went on to swear black-and-blue that it was his Dad and his Dad alone, apart from a little help from above, who brought the drought of '46 to its abrupt end. He swore black-and-blue that it was his Dad and his Dad alone, apart from a little help from above, who brought the floods of '47 to their end. He swore black-and-blue that, when the grasshopper plague of 1950 was headed toward Barmedman, his Dad strode out to the end of the main street. As the advancing plague of insects was about to engulf him, Mr Watson suddenly threw up his hands and every single grasshopper spun around in its tracks and flew away.

So I guess, with an upbringing like that, it was no wonder Wiz was like he was, a bit on the far side of weird and staunchly believing that some of his Dad's powers had rubbed off from father to son, via the Holy Ghost.

We remained far from convinced. Other than a canny ability to hypnotise chooks, we never saw Wiz as capable of performing anything beyond the normal. Though it wasn't for the lack of trying. Once, Jug got Wiz to do his thing with the race form guide. He was at it for hours, mumbling about this, moaning about that, groaning about something else, going into trances, and he still didn't come up with a single winner in either Melbourne, Sydney, Brisbane or Adelaide. Jug and I lost a fortune out of that. Boy were we wild. Jug called Wiz all the names under the sun. Wiz retaliated by putting a curse on Jug so he wouldn't lose his virginity at the next school dance.

That one worked!

Still, Wiz had his uses as a member of our gang. He came in handy when we needed someone to climb through windows and the like. Not that he was the smallest. Bluey was. But we liked Bluey better than Wiz. That's why Wiz ended up with the job. Which was exactly what happened the time Jug agreed to supply a 'poor, lonely, old-age, widowed pensioner' from Leeton with a dozen free-range White Leghorn layers. As delegation was one of Jug's strengths in life, Wiz and I were put in charge of the hen procurement along with the promise of a '10 per cent cut after final sale and ordnance tax'.

The night of the great chook heist proved to be spot on for undercover crime. It was as dark as vegemite. Not even the stars got a look in. After dressing in our overalls and stinkers (sand-shoes) we set out. Down the Mutch House lane and over the channel we went, armed with a torch plus the wheat bags Jug had provided. Around the back of the school hall as quiet as the breeze, and over to the poultry shed where the hens had been locked away for the night.

While we crouched beside the timber and corrugated iron poultry shed taking a breather, I got the strange sense that someone was hovering out there in the pitch darkness. I mentioned it to Wiz. We laid low for a while until he reckoned my imagination was playing tricks. I wasn't so sure. Still, it was too late to turn back. I gave Wiz a heave-ho up under the eves of the poultry shed. He slid beneath the roof and dropped with a light thud. He undid the inside locks and in I crept to join him. The acrid smell of chook shit and feathers bit at my nostrils.

Wiz led the way, cupping the torch so the light wouldn't spray around the place. His hands glowed, X-ray like, translucent red. I could just about see the bones in his fingers. I followed behind carrying the sacks and hanging onto the back of his overalls so as not to trip over. Together we inched our way along between the pens, the wire fencing acting as our guide. The occasional 'Coo . . . Coo . . .' of a slumbering hen caused us to freeze in our tracks. My heart was playing the twenty-one gun salute in my chest. This was crime with a capital 'C'. If we startled the birds, we were as good as gone.

Sweat trickling down my brow, I cursed Jug. I could picture him back in our dorm snoozing contentedly. Just how many times does a bloke have to get the wool pulled over his eyes before he comes to realise that he's nothing but a prize ninny?

'Here,' whispered Wiz when we'd reached the coop we were after. I took the torch. He undid the bolt, then opened the gate. The sound of moving hinges groaned like the door of a haunted house. We stepped into the pen. Chooks clucked about us, gossiping in their sleep. With hardly a breath we nudged our way along to the nests.

'Open a sack.'

It was like taking candy from a baby. I marvelled through the dim light at Wiz's deft touch; the way he'd pluck a sleeping hen off its perch, tuck its head under its wing, rock it back and forward to lull it into a trance, then place it in the sack.

'Next sack.'

I put the sack of hypnotised chooks to one side then went to grab the second sack. I remembered having placed it at my feet.

'The sack.'

'I can't find it. It's on the floor somewhere,' I replied as I took a step backward.

The food trough went over with one almighty crash. In a split second the pen turned into a squawking cacophony. Chooks took off in all directions, scratching, biting, pecking, beating. I tried to make a dash for it but I'd lost all sense of direction. Every step I took was blocked off either by the mass of flying chooks or wire fencing.

Amid the pandemonium the lights came on. All around me was a sea of feathers and dust. I was trapped. Nowhere to run. Nowhere to hide. Helpless, I stood stock still.

When the feathers and dust began to settle, I was still standing there, a sack of chooks hanging from one hand, a torch from the other. At the entrance to the poultry shed stood Ape. Even from that distance the word 'MURDER' was written clearly in his eyes.

Only a miracle could have saved me from this fix. I looked around in search of my accomplice. Lo and behold, Wiz had vanished into thin air.

The Herb

Herbs were the basis of the student market economy. Although strictly forbidden, they were used to strike up deals, win enemies over, buy goods or favours. Plus, they were the currency for the SP and all our other gambling activities. And as was the case in the world outside, where all our role models of film stars and the like smoked, so did we.

There were those amongst us who were confirmed smokers even before they got to Yanco Ag. Meat and 'Horny' Jones reckoned they used to smoke up to ten a day, and 'Slimy' Snodgrass was a chain smoker.

Out of our gang, Slimy was the bloke I least got on with. But due to his reputation as a 'King Herb Rat' he was looked upon, by the younger kids in particular, with utter admiration.

In our first year at school, Slimy was caught and punished for smoking no less than thirty times. But by continuing to smoke he proved beyond all doubt that he had no respect for Dad-ak or the boarding school system. Slimy wore the nicotine stains on his fingers like a defiant brown badge of courage. His smoker's cough barked an ominous presence. His constant ash-like smell became his personal deodorant.

When the younger kids saw Slimy shuffling along they'd gravitate around him. 'How many ya smoked today Slimy?' they'd ask. And Slimy would act almost casual in replying ''Bout twenty or thirty.' The kids would give a gasp. 'Wow!' Then they'd part like the waters of the Red Sea to let Slimy wander off for yet another herb.

I'd smoked before of course; rolled up newspapers, off-cuts of weaving cane and the odd cigarette that I'd pinched from Dad's Ardath packet; but just kid's stuff really. So I asked Slimy to give me smoking lessons.

For the cost of three herbs Slimy conducted his first lesson, aptly titled 'The Draw Back'.

It was held in the tennis shed behind the laundry and tuck shop. I watched with glued attention as Slimy lit a Craven A cork-tipped cigarette. He sucked long, hard and deep. The red glow frittered away into grey ash.

When he eventually finished his drag, Slimy shut his eyes. A look of manly satisfaction spread over his face. He held the smoke down for as long as possible, then exhaled what little remained.

'Your drag,' Slimy said handing over the caved-in herb.

I tentatively took it between the tips of my fingers and drew in until my mouth was full. My face screwed up as the vile smoke burnt at my tongue.

'Now, take a deep breath,' Slimy egged me on.

So I did.

When the smoke hit my lungs, it felt like I'd been bowled over by a steam train. I exploded into spasms of coughs and splutters. I gasped for air. My head went into an uncontrollable spin. I collapsed into a pile of tennis nets. My eyeballs were sucked up inside my brain. I scrambled to the door, stuck my head out and heaved in a succession of violent dry retches.

Yet so determined was I to see the challenge through to its end that I returned to complete lesson one and suffer through another herb. And as I walked back to my dorm feeling as crook as a dog, I took consolation in the knowledge that my life had just taken a giant leap forward and I was knocking on the door of what manhood was really about.

Within a couple of weeks I'd almost conquered the nausea of smoking. After we'd covered the advanced smoker's subjects of 'How to Roll Your Own' and 'The Art of Blowing Smoke Rings', I sacked Slimy as my coach and took to the world as a certified smoker.

The person I modelled myself on was Humphrey Bogart. I copied the slouched walk; the Bogie mumble; the way the cigarette hung from his mouth. I began to imagine that Ingrid

Bergman would appear at the next term school dance. She'd step off the bus from Leeton High School and see me standing under a dim light, surrounded in a foggy cigarette haze. I'd take a long drag on my herb, blow the smoke carelessly in the direction of 'Casablanca', and she'd fall desperately in love with me.

As it happened, I didn't quite make it to that next school dance. Just the night before, as I was puffing away in the toilets perfecting my Bogie impersonation, a hand shot out of the darkness. It grabbed the scruff of my dressing gown and nailed me under a spot of torch light with the evidence still dangling loosely from my lips.

The following morning I faced the full wrath of Dad-ak. I was barred from attending the dance, given six of the best, and then came an almighty lecture. Dad-ak ranted and raved about how nicotine was an addictive drug. He said that smoking was a senseless act only performed by weaklings, imbeciles, idiots and half-wits like myself who were hell-bent on digging themselves into an early grave.

Of course Dad-ak was wrong. Smoking made me feel the complete opposite to everything he said it did. And I certainly didn't give two hoots about being an idiot in Dad-ak's eyes because I knew I'd be a hero in the eyes of the rest of the school, just as Slimy was; just as Bogie was in the eyes of the world.

After I'd been dismissed from Dad-ak's office I went and grabbed a herb from my stash. I raced into the Mutch House toilet block and lit up.

As the smoke bit once more into my lungs, I imagined I was the epitome of the rebel. The tough guy. The smart guy. I was invincible.

'This could be the beginning of a beautiful friendship,' I mumbled, just like Bogie.

Cookie

If there was any one particular animal we had a close affinity with, it was the humble sheep. We were involved in the selection of their breeding; saw them being conceived; witnessed them being born; cared for them as lambs. We marked and mulesed them; dipped and crutched them; practised our slap-dash shearing techniques on them; classed their wool. And, under Cookie's supervision, we eventually butchered them – butchered being the operative word – before they returned to haunt us as the mainstay of our diet.

Yet although we may not have always been satisfied with what Cookie, our one-armed, drunken, ex-Naval chef dished up as main course, it was his dessert, or 'desert' as we called it, which remained our greatest concern.

SUNDAY LUNCH
MAIN COURSE – ROAST LAMB

Not long after rigor mortis had set in, the 'lamb', or scraggy mutton as it was by then, began its life-after-death as Roast Lamb for Sunday lunch. The meat was served with roasted potatoes, pumpkin, carrots, plus peas or beans.

Delivered with our roast lamb came a large stainless steel jug filled to the brim with thick, luke-warm gravy. This we flooded over our dinner. After bolting down the meal, we mopped up the surplus gravy with the plentiful supplies of bread and butter that Cookie provided.

DESSERT – ICE CREAM!!

Ice cream for dessert was a cherished moment. That was the time when a Table Head really had to prove his mettle. The pressure was well and truly on. If he dared give anyone a fraction more than anyone else, the table was likely to erupt into a vicious riot. More friendships were lost over a Sunday plate of ice cream than in any other event at school, including House sport and our term dance.

Ice cream was liquid gold. Most kids, myself included, could hardly control ourselves. As soon as the Table Head passed the bowl, we'd gobble the stuff down. And when we'd eaten all the spoon could scrape out, we'd check that Ma Dad-ak had her back turned before licking the bowl as clean as a whistle.

Other kids, the 'masochists' as we called them, savoured every moment. They waited until the ice cream started to melt. They swirled it around with their spoon. The eyes of the rest of us on the table followed every revolution of that spoon as it twirled its way around and around that thick, creamy, sweet liquid. Then we watched as they ate it in ecstatic slow motion.

We hated the masochists.

SUNDAY NIGHT
MAIN COURSE – ROAST LAMB COLD CUTS

Left-overs from the Sunday roast weren't forgotten. They returned on Sunday night in the form of cold cuts, then reappeared throughout the week for lunch, accompanied by limp salad, cold potatoes, chutney and . . . bread and butter.

DESSERT – PRUNES AND CUSTARD

By Sunday night reality had struck home. Prunes and custard appeared for desert. Their arrival was greeted with a mass groan. The story Jug told us was that Cookie had lost his left arm when the naval ship he was on got torpedoed as he was making a batch of custard. The psychological ramifications of that event had caused long lasting and devastating effects on his custard-making ability.

If the rumour held any truth, it was indeed a cruel twist of fate that we, of all people, were forced to suffer because of the injustices of one man's past tragedies. Excuses of 'Blame it on the Navy' or 'Blame it on the torpedo' or 'Blame it on his one arm' had long been exhausted. Who gave a rat's arse what Cookie's personal problems were when his custard came out a rotten pooey colour, full of indigestible tasteless lumps? To make matters worse, by the time the custard struggled to our table, a leathery skin covered it. This was named the 'Fly Walk'.

Slimy was one of the few kids who could eat the Fly Walk. He reckoned it gave the prunes a smoother ride down into his stomach. The reasoning behind that, we believed, was that Slimy was such a guts he swallowed the prunes, seeds and all. At night, those of us who were unlucky enough to be sitting in the cubicle next to him could just about count the number of prunes he'd eaten by the rattling sound the seeds made when they collided with the side of the dunny bowl.

MONDAY NIGHT
MAIN COURSE – LAMB LOIN CHOPS

The lamb loin chops arrived at our table embalmed in fat. Still, not even that put us off. Loin chops were our favourite. We demolished the meal in a flash before settling back and gnawing contently at the bones, making sure that the marrow had been sucked clean. Then, when every skerrick of meat had disappeared, we'd toss the bones into a communal bowl where they became open slather for anyone else to re-check their potential.

Monday night's meal came with mashed potatoes, boiled carrots, peas or beans, gravy and . . . bread and butter.

DESSERT – PRUNES AND CUSTARD

Monday night's dessert was, much to our regret, a repeat performance of Sunday night.

TUESDAY NIGHT
MAIN COURSE – LAMB STEW

'Lamb spew' was made from off-cuts. It arrived hidden under an inch of solidified fat. But rather than turning us off completely, this had its advantages. It lessened the chances of flies and other foreign bodies drowning in the stew before we got to it.

Lamb spew came with mashed potatoes, carrots, peas or beans and . . . bread and butter.

DESSERT – CUSTARD AND PRUNES

Perhaps Cookie thought that by reversing the wording on the menu, he might bluff us. But we weren't that dumb. However, after a main course of lamb spew, we'd have eaten anything. Well, just about anything. Anything with a bit of sugar in it, that is.

WEDNESDAY NIGHT
MAIN COURSE – LAMB RISSOLES

How Cookie managed to roll the rissoles with one arm was anyone's guess. One rumour suggested that he used the 'armpit method', which explained why they were shaped like mini cow pats. But we refused to let our imaginations ponder on that. Our hunger was too strong. No one ever dared check their rissoles for tell-tale signs of hair.

As luck would have it though, Cookie had a variety of sauces up his (other) sleeve that helped disguise the lamb rissoles. One sauce was a blend of tomato and chutney. Another, a blend of gravy and chutney. The others were blends of both the tomato and chutney and the gravy and chutney sauces.

Lamb rissoles were served with whole boiled potatoes and carrots, mountains of boiled cabbage and . . . bread and butter.

DESSERT – BREAD AND BUTTER PUDDING.

By Wednesday the bread we'd been stuffing ourselves with all week was stale, sometimes mouldy. This caused 'waste not, want not' Cookie to extend his culinary expertise and invent a dish he called . . . bread and butter pudding.

Cookie's bread and butter pudding wasn't anything like the normal bread and butter pudding served on dining room tables throughout Australia. Cookie's pudding was made from custard, topped with the stale, or mouldy, bread then sprinkled with sugar and garnished with more custard.

THURSDAY NIGHT
MAIN COURSE – ROLLED LAMB FLAP OR CRUMBED LAMB CUTLETS

By Thursday the 'lamb' was on the turn. It all came down to just how far the lamb had actually turned. If, as was usual, the egg supply had exhausted itself and we'd already eaten the savoury mince, the lamb's fry, the crumbed brains and the other offerings of offal for breakfast, Thursday night turned out to be a toss-up between crumbed lamb cutlets or rolled lamb flap.

Most of us preferred the cutlets but, because of their rapidly deteriorating condition, they were usually being stewed as a base for Friday and Saturday nights' meals. So, more often than not, it was rolled lamb flap stuffed with Cookie's 'secret seasoning'.

There wasn't much that went on around the place we didn't know about. We loved gossip. So much so that if there wasn't any about, we'd make it up. But when it came to the goings-on in the kitchen, that wasn't necessary. We knew more about Cookie than he knew about himself. We knew where the vanilla essence had vanished. We knew what he and Mona got up to when Mona's husband was off shearing. So naturally enough we knew the recipe to his seasoning. It was only a secret in Cookie's own head. A leak of confidence had occurred somewhere down the track. And apart from the widespread and quite believable suggestion that it was rats' droppings which gave his seasoning that particular taste, we had a fair idea that it was made from eggs, onions, mixed herbs, salt, pepper and stale bread.

The rolled lamb flap – or whatever other lamb dish appeared on a Thursday night – was served with gravy, mashed potatoes, boiled carrots, peas or beans and . . . bread and butter.

DESSERT – PRUNES AND CUSTARD

By Thursday night, Cookie must have begun to worry about our regularity. He returned to the tried and true. The only slight variation was that there seemed to be more prunes floating in the custard on a Thursday than there'd been on Sunday, Monday or Tuesday night. Jug reckoned that the extras might have been cockroaches in disguise. No one could tell. No one could have tasted the difference anyway. But whatever, we all steered clear of Slimy when he visited the dunny on a Thursday night.

FRIDAY NIGHT
MAIN COURSE – LAMB CONTINENTAL

By Friday, the lamb was on the nose. If it'd been allowed to run its normal course, we reckoned that reincarnation would have been well and truly under way. When the wind blew in the wrong direction we could get a ripe whiff of it from over in the school block.

To disguise the smell, Cookie went international. He turned the lamb into what he proudly called 'lamb continental'.

In reality, lamb continental wasn't much more than a cruel attempt at sweet and souring the cutlets that'd been stewed on Thursday. To give it that 'international' flavour Cookie added vinegar, brown sugar and chutney. Apparently pineapple was also added, or so Cookie had once told Jug. But the chances of finding a piece of pineapple in the meal were about the same as taking out first prize in the lottery.

Lamb continental was served with gluggy white rice, boiled carrots, mountains of boiled cabbage, peas or beans and ... bread and butter.

DESSERT – RICE PUDDING

Friday being lamb continental night, the rice theme continued into dessert. Rice pudding was served. But once again, Cookie's version was a recipe all his own, the major ingredient being custard. The minor ingredient, rice, must have been boiled in the custard. Cookie's rice pudding was stodgy at best. At worst it stuck our mouths up like a sickly, sweet glue. When that happened, no one could speak.

SATURDAY NIGHT
MAIN COURSE – LAMB BOMBAY

By Saturday the lamb was on its last legs. Even the school's two sheep dogs kept their distance. Desperate measures had to be taken. To kill the rankness of the meat, Cookie continued with his international theme. In memory of his naval days, when he had almost died a violent death of dysentery, Cookie concocted a dish he christened 'lamb Bombay'.

To the novice, turning the left-over lamb continental into lamb bombay may seem an impossibility. But not to Cookie. He could do wonders with curry. He just about shovelled the stuff into the pot. And when he was satisfied that he'd murdered all the 'off' smells and flavours, he chucked in diced apple, raisins and chutney.

Cookie's lamb Bombay was served with gluggy white rice, boiled carrots, mountains of boiled cabbage, peas or beans and . . . bread and butter.

DESSERT – PRUNES AND CUSTARD

Saturday night we returned to our staple diet. None of us knew what the people in Bombay ate for sweets. Jug reckoned it must have been ice cream, which left us with the responsibility of having eat our way through the world's over-supply of prunes and custard. Still, we ate our dessert, even though we knew what the results would be. By lights out on a Saturday night, the lamb Bombay had met up with the prunes and custard. East had met West, and the two cultures had a violent reaction against each other.

On Saturday night the school's sewerage system was stretched to its limit.

'Galah' Day

'Joe reckons that our "Galah" Day is heaps better 'n the Sydney Royal Easta Show,' Jug boasted, leaning back on his shovel. ''N 'e should know 'cause 'e lives in Kings Cross, right where they hold the Easta Show.'

This was big praise indeed, especially for a such a small agricultural school as ours. None the less, I believed what Jug had said to be true because Gala Day was the most exciting day of the year.

'Hey! You Blokes! Get back to work!' shouted 'Creeping Jesus', the Garden Stock Duties Master.

In a flail of shovels, hoes and forks, Jug, Bluey, Meat and I returned to our attack on the rose gardens. We knew that if we were reported for being slack, we'd be put on the list of Gala Day monitors, regardless of whether our parents were coming or not.

Preparations had begun for our main fund-raising day a month before. To impress our visitors, Dad-ak wanted the place to look perfect. Everyone except the Fifth Years had been drafted onto extra Stock Duties. Dairy, piggery and poultry areas had been scrubbed. Produce from the vegie gardens and orchard was being picked and stored in the cold room to await sale. The school block was getting cleaned. The oval was being mowed. The tractors and implements had been washed. The silage area behind the dairy was tidied. And we were re-re-weeding the gardens.

Down on the oval, the tractor slalom course had been marked out. For a small charge, anyone's skill could be tested by threading the International WD 40 through a line of flags while dragging a tractor tyre attached to a length of rope. The shearing shed was ready for shearing and wool classing demonstrations. Logs had been trucked in for the Yanco/Wamoon Wood Chopping Championships; an area marked out for gum boot throwing. For those who always travelled with their dogs, we had erected temporary fencing and had provided a few ewes and wethers for sheep dog trials.

After our stint in the gardens, we built a special enclosure on the oval for the 'Guess the Bull's Weight' competition. There was just one problem: the star himself, Brutus. He refused to budge from his pen.

'How 'bout we get a heifer that's in season. That might get 'im movin',' Jug suggested.

So we did. Meat led the heifer, tantalisingly, past the open gate of Brutus's pen. The instant Brutus caught a whiff, his eyes lit up. He rose to his full height, let out a deafening bellow and took off after that heifer with his balls flopping around like excited sacks of flour.

'Get that bloody cow movin'!' Jug called out.

Us kids pulled, pushed, bashed and belted the heifer. But to no avail. She was as keen on getting together with Brutus as Brutus was with her. Before we got anywhere near the enclosure, Brutus had mounted her.

'Ow can we stop 'em Jug?' Bluey asked.

'There's no stoppin' 'em once they're as excited as that,' Jug replied.

And he was right.

Meanwhile, on the lawns outside McCaughey House an assortment of tents had been rising like mushrooms. There were tents where the school produce was to be sold, a caterers' tent, boxing tent, first aid tent, parents and citizens tent and the old boys' produce tent.

For any little kids who came along there was a merry-go-round. A forty-four-gallon drum of water was set up for the youngsters to try and catch tin fish on a line which had a magnet tied to its end. There was hoop-la, lucky dips and a chocolate wheel.

Near the pump shed by the lake, an open-topped corrugated

iron tank was filled with water in readiness for 'Dunk the Teacher'. 'Drown the Nit' we called it. Here, the teachers took turns at perching on a plank above the tank. At the side, a paddle was hooked up to a release rope. When someone threw a soft-ball and hit the paddle, the plank gave way, plunging the Nit into the water.

Drown the Nit was our favourite. It was the only time we could wreak our revenge on the Nits and get away with it. Ape was the main target. When he sat on the plank, the queue almost reached the Mutch House lane. Everyone in that line was fired up. You could see it in their eyes; feel it in the air. When Ape got dunked, the cheers just about rocked the foundations of McCaughey House.

'Nobby' Napier, the oldest surviving Old Yanconian, or Old Boy as we called them, came on the Friday to set up his dilapidated toffee apple caravan next to the Bunya pine on the lake's edge. Just as Nobby had settled in, the Giacomini brothers arrived and erected their flash fairy floss van beside Nobby's wreck. The rivalry between old Nobby and the Giacomini brothers was intense. Being an Old Boy, Nobby got most of our sympathy, if not most of our custom.

'Never trust no bugger whose name ya can't pronounce,' Nobby always warned.

Those words of wisdom caused many of us to go into hard training, trying to pronounce 'Giacomini' so we'd feel better about buying fairy floss behind Nobby's back. For weeks before Gala Day kids could be seen walking around, contorting their lips as if attempting camel impersonations. But they weren't. They were day-dreaming about fairy floss, and that had triggered them off into silently wrestling with that almost unpronounceable name.

'How's it goin' Meat?'

'Gi . . . a . . . com . . . i . . . n . . . i.'

Dad-ak was in his element on the Friday before Gala Day. He strode around the place like a general with a pack of 'slackers' at his heel. When he saw anything untoward he barked, 'Paper!'

or, 'Weed!' and the slackers scurried out from behind his legs to dive on whatever it was, as if their lives depended on it.

By pre-lights out flicker we were completely exhausted from our long day's labours. But if anyone was expecting a good night's sleep, they were in for a big disappointment.

After lights out, Jug and I lay in our beds waiting for the Annual Dorm Raid from the group of Old Boys who'd spent Friday priming themselves at Yanco Pub. At some ungodly hour we heard their cars roar down the drive. They screeched to a halt outside McCaughey House.

'Into the dunnies!' Jug sounded the alarm around the dorm.

We scampered into the toilets as the wild and reckless daredevils pounded up the stairs. Into our dorm they came, upending beds and lockers before fleeing back to the sanctuary of the pub. We were left quaking in our cotton pyjamas, packed like sardines in the cubicle.

On the morning of Gala Day we sorted out the previous night's mess before receiving a special allocation of pocket money. Then we helped load up the stalls before returning to our dorms to make them spick and span.

Because Dad-ak was so busy, our Dorm Prefects were given the responsibility to make certain that everything was immaculate, including ourselves. They checked that beds had been made with nurse's corners; school uniforms were clean; school ties were done in the unfathomable double windsor knot; shoes had been spit-and-polished.

'Got clean underdaks on Meat?' our Dorm Prefect, 'Muscles' Meakin, asked.

'Not sure,' replied Meat meekly.

'Well make sure! What if ya have an accident 'n end up in hospital?'

Which left Meat pondering as to what the connection was between him having clean underpants, and having an accident and ending up in hospital.

'But, I don't wear none most'a the time, Swampy. It saves on the washin'.'

After inspection, the slackers drifted to their allotted posts. Some went down to the oval to act as parking monitors; others to the boxing tent. The waiters went to the catering tent, ready to take orders for tea and scones. The tour guides gathered at the front entrance of McCaughey House.

'Gee, whad if a couple'a good lookers want the full guided tour?'

'Blimey. That'd be good, eh?'

'Never know ya luck, eh?'

Apart from old Nobby, who spend the night guarding his toffee apple caravan just in case the Giacomini brothers set fire to it, Jug's brother Joe was the first of the Old Boys to arrive. Even though he'd tossed in the hectic life of a farmer to go in search of 'the big quid', Joe hadn't missed a Gala Day since he'd been a student during the war. Joe arrived looking like he'd just come out of an American gangster film, parking his flashy car next to the NO PARKING sign outside McCaughey House.

'How's it goin' little brotha,' he greeted Jug, ''n how's me 'ol mate Swamp?'

Joe never got my nickname right. But it didn't matter. Just to be included as Joe's mate was enough for me.

Jug and I acted as Joe's assistants. While we were unloading the SP and setting it up out of sight around the back of the boxing tent, Joe told us about life in Kings Cross.

'Cor she was a goer little brotha, I tell ya,' Joe said as he was patching the radio through to the boxing tent. 'A dancer she was, Swamp. On 'er way ta Lost Vague-iss. Done me like a dinner she did. Woke up in the mornin' red raw 'n she'd taken me last brass razoo.'

Parents were the first visitors to arrive, keen to be reunited with their sons. We felt sorry for the kids whose families came to Gala Day. It spoilt it for them. They were never able to enjoy the day as much as the rest of us. They had to sit on a woollen blanket in family groups, eat from picnic hampers and answer tricky questions.

'Well son, what have you got to say about this maths report of yours?'

It was strange to see those kids looking so different with their parents around. Slimy could have almost been mistaken for a blue-and-gold cherub. But we knew more about him than his parents did. We knew all the strife he'd been in; how he'd been caught smoking a couple of nights ago and was still on detention after being nabbed raiding the kitchen.

The last to roll up were the Old Boys. They drifted in around noon looking the worse for wear from their previous night's reunion. Jug and I awaited the Old Boys arrival eagerly. Some were living legends, and the stories told about their colourful deeds had become part of the school's folklore.

These blokes were the real school heroes, far removed from those whose names hung in dull gold leaf on the honour boards of scholastic achievement around the walls of the school hall. These were real blokes; the ones who'd come face to face with adversity and had conquered it.

'See that bloke?' Joe pointed. 'That's "Cruncher" Connell. He once flattened 'alf 'a Wagga's first grade footy team after one of 'em called him a poof.

''N the bloke next'a 'im. That's "Klappers" Kimber, 'e got expelled after gettin' two sheilas up the duff. Both of 'em on the night'a the same school dance.

''N the bloke with 'em, well 'e's "Viking" Petersen. A diver 'e was. They reckon 'e once did five somersaults off the Euroley Bridge with a broken arm 'e got tryin' ta do the exact same thing jus' the week before.'

Jug and I gasped in awe. We sidled up to the group while they were having a chat.

'G'day Klappers,' Jug butted in.

'You Joe's young brotha are ya?'

'Yeah.'

''Ope ya not as full'a piss 'n wind as 'e is,' Klappers laughed.

And Jug and I walked off feeling ten feet tall at having spoken with one of Yanco Ag's great legends.

By early afternoon everyone had arrived. Almost two hundred people turned up on the day. So while all the activities down on the oval were in full swing, the lawns outside McCaughey House were also swarming.

A bloodthirsty roar echoed out of the boxing tent; a sign that someone had been floored by a 'haymaker'. Jug and I rushed around to watch the blood-splattered 'Owl' Wise being taken to Ma Dad-ak in the first aid tent.

Joe had organised for the bouts to be slotted in between horse races so everyone had time to lay their bets and hear the call. Though the SP was highly illegal, Dad-ak turned a blind eye. That was probably because it was the best money earner of the day, although it could have been a lot more profitable if Joe hadn't pocketed the odd fiver. 'Jus' ta cover me expenses,' as he put it.

By mid-afternoon the Old Boys had recovered enough to tackle the keg that Joe had hidden in the pump shed by the lake. Then, after all the scheduled and unscheduled fights plus the day's racing program had been completed, the boxing tent gave way to 'Catch the Greasy Pig'.

At any time a greasy pig is a hard thing to latch on to, but with a few beers under the belt, bedlam reigned supreme. The rule was that the person who finally captured the pig could take it home. But because everyone was having so much fun they never did. Once caught, the pig was immediately donated back to the school. Within minutes it was re-greased and they were at it again.

After half an hour the Old Boys were completely knackered. So was the pig. It squatted in the corner, shaking like a newt. The men huffed and puffed as they looked the pig over. The pig sort of looked back at the men.

'Wad'da ya reckon fellers?' Cruncher wheezed. 'Time fer a beer?'

Then, with the two sides satisfied a good contest had been run, a truce was called. The blokes gathered up the pig and took it over to the beer keg in the pump shed, where they had a few more pick-me-ups.

'Here's ta the pig!' Viking toasted.

'Here's!'

And they up-ended their disguised mugs while the pig slurped contently at the special bucket of beer slops that the Old Boys had provided.

Amongst all these goings-on the women weren't forgotten. They took part in chook plucking competitions, knitting and crochet competitions, jam tastings, sniff the herb competitions. There were prizes for the best scones, biscuits and cakes.

Though we weren't involved in anything the women were up to, Jug and I kept an eager eye out for when the food judging was over. It was then that we could stoke up our ravenous stomachs. And what top-class grub it was, cooked mostly by the wives of Old Boys. Good wholesome bush cooking. It had to be, else we could think of no other reason why an Old Boy would want to give up his wild, carefree ways to become snared into marriage.

By tea-time the tents were sold out and Jug and I were starving again. Dinner was held in the dining room and was open to all. Tables were set in long rows and the food placed out for people to help themselves. If any student was caught bogging in before our guests, he'd be ordered to report to 'Rock-Jaw' the following morning and be caned for bad manners. So we circled the dining room like a polite pack of vultures, waiting patiently to swoop and demolish what was left.

'Same tucker every bloody year,' Joe grumbled.

From our experience the Gala Day menu hadn't changed. Cookie always served a main course of cold lamb and salad. For dessert there was the rare treat of trifle – light on rum because he'd drunk most of it – plus the usual serve of lumpy custard.

While everyone was at tea, Dad-ak and a few of his favoured students – 'sucks' as we called them – were out on the main islet setting up the fireworks display. As the sun set, everyone began taking vantage points around the lake's edge and along the veranda.

'Gonna be a ripper this year,' Meat whispered excitedly. 'Overheard Dad-ak sayin' that 'e's got lots'a new stuff. Ya not ta tell tho'. It's a secret.'

'Ya not kiddin'?'

'That's wot I heard.'

'Hey fellers. Did ya hear what Meat reckons?'

After all was set, Dad-ak appeared on the bridge. Even though it was near on dark I could still feel his presence. Apart from the drunken pig's slurred oinking, belching and farting, a hush fell over the place, adults and children alike. Dad-ak thanked our visitors for coming and everyone for their efforts. Then he called out the words we'd been waiting the whole year to hear.

'Let the fireworks begin!'

And it was an absolute blinder. Rockets shot miles into the sky exploding into cascades of coloured waterfalls. There were lady crackers and star lights. There were things that whooshed, whizzed and wobbled; cannons, volcanoes, Roman candles and myriads of pops, gargles, bangs, spurts and sparkles.

The actual display went for fifteen to twenty minutes. And although the intoxicated pig scuttled off to escape shell-shock, every man, woman and child remained riveted to the spot. Even the Old Boys were held spellbound. Viking stood gazing up into the sky, rocking groggily back and forward, completely unaware of the mug of beer he held precariously in his hands.

At the height of the display Joe reckoned that the fireworks could be seen all the way over in Narrandera. By the time the last fizzer had fizzed its last, a thick, dense, black fog of gunpowder had settled around the lawns, clogging my lungs and making Viking screw up his face as he guzzled down the last of his beer.

After the display, Jug and I helped Joe pack away the SP.

'See ya later little brotha,' Joe said. 'Same to you Swamp.'

Just as he was about to drive off, he slipped us a few packs of herbs as payment for our day's labours.

'Look after ya self Joe,' Jug called.

'''N don't let them women wear ya down too much,' I added.

'If only they would,' Joe replied with a wink, before taking off in a screech of tyres.

As us students prepared for bed, the highlights of the day were the topic of conversation. Not a word was mentioned about the massive Emu Parade and clean-up to follow.

'Where d'ya reckon that drunk pig's ran off ta?' Bluey asked, full of concern.

'Dunno. But sure as hell it's gonna 'ave a doozey of a hangover be tomorra,' came Meat's reply.

Then it was lights out. As I slipped between the sheets, Jug's boastful words about our Gala Day being better than the Sydney Royal Easter Show sprang to mind. And in those final flickering moments before sleep I was washed with a wave of pride, knowing that we'd put on a show better than those city slickers.

Well Above the Average

During Prep one evening, Horny was flipping through his latest girlie magazine when he stumbled across a statistic which stated that the average length of the erect male penis was six-and-a-half inches. No other piece of information in all our days of schooling made such an immediate and long-lasting impact.

That night after Prep not a single ruler remained in our classroom, nor the next night, nor the one after that. Soon it became standard practice that the last thing we did before leaving Prep was to slip our rulers under our shirts and smuggle them back to our dorm in readiness for the night's activities.

After placing the ruler strategically under our pillow, we prepared for bed, our minds filled with hope that during the last twenty-four hours a miracle of gigantic proportions had taken place. By pre-lights out flicker the expectant atmosphere in the dorm was almost unbearable.

When the Duty Nit turned out the lights there was instant silence. For about ten minutes the dorm lay as still as a graveyard. Then, almost as if in the far distance, the gentle jangling of someone's wire sprung bed began to sound. Like a call to arms from the angel Gabriel we began to chime in. From one bed to the other the noise gathered intensity. Soon we'd all be going flat out. As the racket of galloping springs peaked, we struck a problem. There was only one torch to go round.

'TORCH!' came the desperate call out of the darkness.

The bloke who had the torch dashed across the dorm to the caller. With his ruler at the ready the caller snatched the torch from under his mosquito net like a relay baton. He whipped the sheet and blanket over his head to hide from view, plunged the ruler as deep as possible into his groin to gain that all-important last eighth of an inch, then turned on the torch to take the measurement.

'Eight-and-a-half inches!' he sang out in audible disbelief.

'Bull shit,' the chorus echoed back.

Each night we went through the same ritual. Those of us who were below the average stuck faithfully to the basic principle of physics which stated 'the more you pull at something, the more likely it is to stretch.' And the male ego, being what it is, caused those who were already longer than the average to want to be even longer still.

Yet we believed that as long as we didn't shoot the bolt we'd remain safe from the horrors of hairs growing on the palms of our hands, warts covering our bodies, walking pigeon-toed, or worse still, going blind.

But it wasn't easy to take yourself to the limit and be satisfied with a mere measurement, no matter what the reading. Sometimes we'd forget about the ruler under our pillow, or how well we stacked up against the male population. Before we could shout 'TORCH' our imaginations got the better of us and we'd start having a sexual fantasy.

My fantasies were mostly about Mona, the school's kitchen maid. I'd be sitting alone, starving hungry, in the vast dining room, when she'd appear. She always wore a huge pair of fluffy pink slippers ten times too big for her feet. Other than the slippers she'd be as naked as the girls in the magazines Horny kept hidden in his locker; right between his school jumper and his shirts, on the top left side of the shelf, next to his singlets.

When Mona arrived, the faint smell of naphthalene wafted through the air. She'd climb up on the table like a sensual feast.

I'd always had a strange fascination about Mona's breasts, even when she was fully-clothed. But when they lay within grasp like two bowls of deliciously vibrating jelly, it all became too much. I wouldn't have given two hoots about hairs growing on the palm of my hands, or warts, or walking pigeon-toed. And if, at that moment, I'd been given the choice of going blind or not, I'd have preferred blindness. When all's said and done, what full-blooded bloke would even wish for sight if all he had to look down at was a four-and-a-half inch penis?

But when the images of Mona had been exhausted, the guilt returned.

Then one Sunday night Horny arrived back from weekend leave with some astounding news. His Dad had told him that what we were doing was completely normal; an act performed by the vast majority of males. With us attending an all boys boarding school he was surprised we hadn't been at it long ago.

When Horny mentioned the horrible things we'd heard it'd do, his Dad reckoned that those who'd made up that sort of garbage probably masturbated more than the rest of us put together. And though it was only one adult voice in the wilderness, we latched on to Horny's Dad's words.

It was as if we'd suddenly been freed from a life sentence of frustration and guilt. We pooled our pocket money and bought two more torches. We pinched graph paper from the Maths room. Each of us drew up our own Erection Chart on which we plotted our measurements.

As incentives, Jug decided that prizes should be given to the longest, the most improved, and a special encouragement award for the shortest.

At the end of the year Jug collected our charts. Lo and behold, when he worked it out, our dorm average was seven inches, an amazing half-an-inch above the statistics for the entire male population of the world!

Brimming with pride, we announced the news to the rest of the kids in our class. But they weren't impressed. The blokes from Suck's dorm reckoned that they'd been doing the same experiment and their dorm average was seven-and-a-quarter inches; a quarter-of-an-inch above ours. Then the blokes from the other dorm reckoned that their average was a massive seven-and-a-half inches.

Mind you, Jug and I were of the mind that they might have been stretching things just a bit too much.

The Shadow of 'Dangerous Des' and 'Gorilla' Crowley

If anything was sacred at school, it was Rugby League football. Everyone got involved. The Nits became referees and coaches; kids who couldn't play helped out as strappers, linesmen, ball boys or coach's assistants.

Jug and I lived and breathed sport. While we'd become restless within minutes of a school lesson, we'd willingly sit for hours listening to Joe talk about Yanco Ag's great footy deeds.

But then Joe had a way of telling a story.

'Yanco Ag's first footy capt'n was "Dangerous" Des McAuliffe. The game was down near the Euroley Bridge Road. They were up against a gang'a railway fettlers, half of 'em on the run from the law. Next to the fettlers our blokes looked out'a place. "Easy beats" 'n "Bush babies" the fettlers tagged 'em. But by the end'a the day when "Gorilla" Crowley crashed over ta score the winnin' try, with two murderers hangin' off 'im like wet rags, them fettlers knew different.

'But what them fettlers didn't realise, Swamp, is that Yanco Ag came out'a hardships. Right from the word go they reckoned Sir Sam McCaughey 'ad lost 'is marbles 'cause 'e reckoned 'e could turn dry farmin' land into an oasis with irrigation. But 'e didn't give up, Swamp, not on ya life. 'N 'e done it. 'E showed 'em good and proper, 'ol Sir Sam did.

''N then after Sir Sam died 'n gave 'is land ta the Gov'n'ment, they weren't gonna turn it into a school like 'e wanted. They were broke; down the gurgler. They wanted ta sell it lock, stock 'n barrel ta pay off their debts.

''N then along came a bloke called Mutch. 'E was like us, Swamp. Salt'a the earth. 'E'd been a roustabout, see. None of that cushy stuff, sittin' 'round parliament fer 'im. Old Mutchie, well 'e knew farmers, 'n 'e'd seen 'em fight drought, 'n flood, 'n plagues 'n stuff. 'N 'e reckoned if anyone could get this here school up 'n runnin' it'd be the kids'a them cockies.

'So, in early '22, the school's first Headmaster, Ernest Breakwell, 'n his missus, started out to the place they were gonna turn into Yanco Ag. There was a drought at the time, 'n bush fires had burned most'a the bridges from Hay to Sir Sam's old place. Them two 'ad ta swim across channels full'a leeches 'n stuff, jus' ta get 'ere. 'N when they did, it was a mess, Swamp. Poor ol' Mrs Breakwell jus' broke down 'n cried she did. The place was full'a weeds 'n snakes. There was no water, no lights, no ice chest, no stove fer cookin'. 'N the next week, with the tempratcha nudgin' 120 in the water bag, up the drive troops the small band'a Nits, 'n kids, 'n staff.

'But the thing was, Swamp, no one gave up. Not even when the kid got drowned in the river, they didn't. No one said, "Bugger it. This's too 'ard. Let's pack up and go 'ome." Not on ya life they didn't, Swamp.

'Everyone got stuck in to do their bit. None'a this complainin' lark that ya see these days. Ol' Breakwell, well 'e reckoned that blokes with guts were jus' as good as blokes with brains. 'N by the end of the first year, Yanco Ag mightn't'a been able ta boast a crop'a bright sparks, but what it could boast was a bunch'a kids who'd turned fourteen acres'a scrub into vegie gardens, crops 'n orchards. 'N more importantly Swamp, because'a blokes like Dangerous Des 'n Gorilla Crowley, Yanco Ag was the most feared footy team in the area.

' 'N though youse blokes got it much easier than Dangerous and Gorilla, ya know how they felt. Blokes like you 'n me brotha also gotta work the soil 'n look after the stock. 'N youse got 'omesick like they did. I know Swamp, 'cause young Jug tol' me. So like Dangerous 'n Gorilla ya gotta stick together like ya lives depend upon it. That's what mates are about, Swamp. That's what Yanco Ag's about. That's what footy's about, stickin' together.'

Bread and Jam

A dark night, well after lights out. Jug and I get out of our beds. We stuff clothes, towels, anything we can find, under our blankets so it looks like we're still asleep.

Softly across the lino floor, like natives stalking their prey; over to the double doors of our Mutch House dorm. We check along the veranda, this way and that. All is still. Only the sounds of sleep can be heard. Meat bursts into a choking snore. We freeze. He stops. We venture on along the veranda to the top of the stairs. The chilly night air rushes to greet us. With it comes the smells of the kitchen. The smell of food. So close, yet so far.

Down the stairs. Step by precarious step we descend as light as butterflies, our feet in unison to balance the weight across the loose boards.

We have done this often; so often in fact that there's no need for words. We have perfected it, almost. A mistake! The CREAK of a loose board echoes down the corridor, past the Duty Nit's room. The light is still on. There is silence within. The Duty Nit must be doing his rounds. Who is it tonight? Tyson Tynan and Ten Quid Frobisher, I think. We know it isn't Ape. No one raids the kitchen when Ape is on duty. He gives you six of the best and that's before he sends you to Dad-ak. There you get another serve plus a stint on detention, cleaning the kumbungi out of the channels or some other grotty job. That's if you're lucky. Moof McTavish was almost expelled after he was caught with a loaf of bread in his hands and a cooked chook stuffed down the front of his pyjama pants.

Across to the dining room door. Out with the key. It's the cheapest key to hire because it fits the door nearest the Duty Nit's room. 'Tight-arse' Timms charged us a packet of herbs just for the night. Then we had to fork out another ten herbs for the keys to the larder, the butter safe and the bread store. It's an expensive business, satisfying our hunger.

'One'a these days we're gonna own every single one'a them keys, ourselves, Swampy,' Jug swears each time we plan a kitchen raid.

In the dark I have difficulty getting the key into its hole. My hands are sweaty. I can't grip properly. The key slips. It falls to the floor like a sledge hammer breaking glass.

'Shit!' Jug says.

We shuffle about in desperate search. Footsteps sound in the distance, along the Mutch House veranda. They're heading toward the stairs we've just descended. I start to panic.

'Got it!' whispers Jug.

The footsteps are getting closer. Jug clatters about noisily. The door to the dining room swings open. We dive inside, close the door and crouch down. The footsteps descend the stairs. We dare not breathe. It doesn't sound like Ten Quid or Tyson. Torch light flashes over-head like a lighthouse beacon. The steps disappear into the Duty Nit's room. We heave a sigh of relief.

On all fours we navigate past tables and chairs to the kitchen. Up the slight ramp. We know the layout like the back of our hands. Automatically Jug heads for the larder and butter safe; me for the bread store and cutlery drawer. I rummage about, returning to meet Jug by the stainless steel work bench at the centre of the kitchen. We saw off inch-thick slices of bread, lather them with creamy butter, and ply on the jam. It's strawberry tonight. Our favourite. We slap together two massive sandwiches each. We start to make a third.

There comes a rattling from the unlocked dining room door, our only avenue of escape. A Nit enters. His torch plays this way and that.

'Who's there?' comes the call.

It's Ape! What's he doing here? We stuff our sandwiches into our pyjama tops and take cover under the kitchen sink.

Ape enters the kitchen. Jug and I squash ourselves in amongst the sink piping; out of sight, we hope. The torch spots the mess on the table. The jar with its top off, the unwrapped butter, the bread knife hanging like a dagger from the loaf of bread.

'Little bastards! I'll ring your scrawny necks!'

Ape finds the light switch. The lights snap on. If he looks this way we're goners. I shut my eyes tight. 'Dear God if you can get me out of this mess I'll never ever go on another kitchen raid, not in my whole life. Cross my heart and hope to die.'

There comes a scratching noise from above. Someone's outside the kitchen window.

'Shit Rags! Ape's in the bloody kitchen!'

It's Moof. Ape spins around. The clatter of garbage tins ring out like bell chimes from heaven.

'Let's get out'a here!' shouts Rags.

Theirs is the most untidy escape in history – crashing garbage bins, stamping feet, tripping, falling, panicked voices. Ape runs to the kitchen door. It's locked. He takes off back through the dining room and out of the door he'd entered – the door we'd entered. Down the corridor he gallops, into the Mutch House lane and away in the direction of McCaughey House.

He's gone!

Jug and I take off like emus. Through the dining room we scamper, clutching onto our pyjama tops, holding the sandwiches. In three leaps and a bound we reach the top of the stairs. Like lightning we're back in our dorm. We toss the stuffing out of our beds. We dive in and yank our blankets over our heads, tight.

My heart sounds like an elephant dancing on top of an empty forty-four gallon drum. The sweet smell of jam fogs my lungs. I lay as still as a corpse, petrified that Ape will trace us.

But he doesn't.

'Swampy! Swampy! I reckon it's safe now,' comes Jug's

welcome voice. I slip out of my cocoon and suck in the night air. It injects me with life.

Propping ourselves up in our beds, Jug and I extricate our battered and bruised sandwiches. Jam sticks to our chests, but we don't care.

'Here's to Ape!' Jug says, as we tuck in with huge greedy bites.

A Trip into Town

The throng pressed hard against our Sports Master, 'Flash' Tony Merino, as he pinned the weekend footy teams onto the notice board.

'"Bull" Brady's in,' someone shouted.

We all cheered.

Bull was Yanco Ag's First Grade captain. Jug's hero, and mine. We'd once seen him in a game where three blokes had a go at him. There was blood everywhere. Flash tried to drag him from the field, but Bull wouldn't budge. In the end Ma Dad-ak wrapped a bandage around his head and Bull went on to lead his team to victory with a depressed fracture of the cheek bone and half his right ear ripped off.

'Thought Bull'd done 'is hammy?' Slimy asked.

'Bull'd play with a broken leg if he 'ad ta,' Jug replied.

For this coming Saturday, as usual, we were all in the same team to play at Leeton. Jug was our captain. Meat was our strength, though he had to have salt baths to lose some weight. Bluey and I had the opposite problem. We were too light, so Jug put rocks in our side pads at the weigh-ins.

Soon only a small group of kids remained around the notice board, most of them leaders of different gangs. They'd stayed behind to sort out some important business. Rags nodded at the Fifth and Fourth Year gang leaders; Jug at the Second and Third Year leaders.

'My gang'll give it a bash,' Jug said, and off we wandered.

At Yanco Ag, a trip into town was more than just a chance to pit our sporting might against other schools. It also proved an ideal opportunity to replenish our dwindling stocks of herbs. As with any of our illicit activities, the purchase and the smuggling operation were highly organised.

After the news spread that our gang had agreed to buy herbs for the Second and Third Years, things hotted up. Money started changing hands under stairwells, behind doors, in toilets and anywhere else we least expected to be sprung.

By the end of Friday night's Prep we had over thirty blokes wanting to buy cigarettes.

Jug drew up two lists. The first was to stay at school. It contained the names of the buyers and what they wanted to purchase. The second list was written in code so that it couldn't be used as evidence. This was the list which was to be taken into town. It read, '20 Hungry Corks', (twenty packets of Craven 'A' Cork Tip); '10 Grasshoppers' (ten packets of Turf), and '15 Bark Huts' (fifteen packets of Log Cabin).

The following morning before we left school an important ritual took place. All of us except Jug drew straws to decide who was going to be the 'Pigeon'.

Bluey drew the shortest straw. As Pigeon he became responsible for the purchase and safe conduct of the herbs. He hid the money on himself, plus the coded buying list, then we went to get our names checked off by the Duty Nit as we boarded the bus.

'Good mornin' Mister Tynan,' Jug spruiked. 'Nice day fer it, eh?'

'Maybe, Ashton. Maybe,' 'Tyson' replied with a hint of suspicion.

Due to the system of privileges, the seating arrangements on the bus were predetermined. The oldest were first on, first off, and sat down the back. The youngest, being the last on and last off, had the seats up the front near the Duty Nit, who sat next to the bus driver.

The logic of the seating arrangements was simple. The greater the distance between a kid and the Duty Nit, the less were his chances of getting caught while having an early morning puff or getting up to any other mischief that might relieve the boredom of the trip.

When we arrived at the Leeton football grounds, Tyson

stood outside the bus to mark us off again. Why all this double checking no one seemed to know. Jug once reckoned the Nits may have thought that, in our enthusiasm at throwing as much stuff as possible out the bus window, we might also have mistakenly hoiked a few kids out as well.

Because of the size of the Leeton football ovals not all our teams could play at the one time. The first thing we did was to find out when our game was on. Luckily we were to play early, so we knew we could use thirst as an excuse to ask permission to go up to town.

After our game Bluey, acting like he'd just spent the last month lost in the desert, approached Tyson.

'Please Sir,' he gasped. 'I'm as thirsty as Burke and Wills. May I go up the street 'n get a drink?'

What Bluey omitted from his well-mannered request was that, while he was asking permission for himself, he was also asking – sort of – if the rest of us could tag along.

To save any misunderstanding, once Tyson had okayed Bluey's request, we all tried to make a discreet exit from the ovals. After grabbing our bags and school blazers, Jug and I drifted off nonchalantly in a northerly direction, Bluey headed south, Slimy east, and Meat west. As soon as we were out of sight, we doubled back to meet at a designated spot.

We never dealt with tobacconists. To walk into a tobacconist to buy herbs was a dead give-away. But we knew of three or four shopkeepers who wouldn't dob us in or refuse our service.

After lobbing at Leo's Orange Spot we gathered outside in case there were any last minute hitches. At Yanco Ag individualism was never our forte. As we worked, studied, played, ate, showered and shared a dorm together, the mere thought of just *one* of the gang entering a shop seemed strange. So after a final check that the coast was clear, we all barged in through the front door.

Leo, realising why we'd entered, rushed to serve his customers before any business took place. He had his reputation to uphold. We respected that. In order not to look suspicious we made ourselves as inconspicuous as possible. Bluey began browsing through the magazine rack. Slimy studied the price of the baked beans. Jug and I sat down at the table, pretending to wait for service. And Meat stood up against the side wall attempting to look invisible.

It was just as well that Leo was aware of our method of approach. Otherwise, he'd have thought that a hold-up was on the cards. I'm sure his customers did. Some looked very nervous. But they couldn't have been further off the mark. Theft was very much against the grain at Yanco Ag, and the last thing we wanted was to harm such an important business relationship.

As the last of the customers scurried from the shop, Leo placed a BACK IN TEN MINUTES sign out the front. This was the cue for Bluey to make his move toward the counter. The rest of us, not wanting to miss out on the transaction, gravitated there with him.

'Could I help you with something?' Leo asked, knowing full well what we were after.

Bluey leant over, cupped his hand to his mouth and whispered in his best counter-espionage voice, 'Herbs.'

Pondering the moral issues of selling cigarettes to school kids, Leo's face took on a grim look. When he'd satisfied himself that pounds, shillings and pence boosted his bank balance more than morals did, he agreed to see the order.

Bluey stepped back from the counter and we formed a tight ring around him. This allowed him some privacy while he fished in the depths of his underpants for the order and cash. After all had been accounted for, we parted and Bluey handed over the coded order and the money.

Leo's eyes sparkled at the size of the order. He headed out to the back where his bulk stocks were kept. The rest of us tagged along. As Leo and Bluey filled the order, they passed the cartons to Jug, who broke them up and gave them to us to stash away into our secret hiding spots.

The best hiding place was inside the lining of our school blazers. Another was the false bottom of a carry bag. A packet of smokes could squeeze down into the toes of a football boot before being covered over with a smelly sock to deter Nits from prying. Our underpants were also a good hiding spot, because Nits were wary about checking near our private parts for fear of innuendo.

Jug never carried herbs. No gang leaders did. His major part in the operation was yet to come. After the rest of us stashed away the herbs, we returned to the sports oval, attempting to walk as normally as possible.

'McFadyen, why are you limping like that?' Tyson called.

'Got a bit of a corkie, sir.'

'You'd better see Matron when we get back to school.'

'Yes, sir.'

We breathed a sigh of relief.

There was a lot riding on the safe return of this contraband. Herbs were of a far greater value in the school than they were on the outside. The amount of tension on the return trip was directly related to just who the Duty Nit was, and what sort of mood he was in. Usually we disguised our anxiety by mucking around and making as much racket as possible.

Unlike other schools, we weren't noted singers on bus trips. It was only on the odd occasion we'd relax and allow the revelry to overflow into song. Then we'd rip into our repertoire of favourites like, 'Nothing could be finer than to be in her vagina every mor-or-or-ning', or, 'Dina, Dina, show us your leg, a yard above your knee'.

Still, every man and his dog knew that in the history of Yanco Agricultural High School there hadn't been a single bus trip where an attempt to smuggle cigarettes back into school hadn't been made. The Nits knew this. They also knew that, if they didn't catch at least a couple of kids, Dad-ak would haul them over the coals for being too lenient. So it had become an unwritten law that a few kids had to get caught. There had to be a sacrifice. And that's where the Pigeons from each smuggling gang fulfilled their obligations.

As we prepared to file off the bus, Bluey placed a packet of herbs in the top pocket of his blazer, where the outline could clearly be seen. Tyson, checking us off the bus, naturally saw the cigarettes.

'Johnson. What have we here, son.'

'Nothin' Sir.'

'Looks like a packet of cigarettes to me.'

'Yes, Sir.'

'Have you got any more?'

'Not sure, Sir.'

While Tyson was busy searching Bluey, Jug, who didn't have any herbs on him, spoke up.

'The natives are gettin' restless sir. Would ya like me ta check a few of 'em off while ya busy with Bluey?'

Tyson, aware of the grumbling bottleneck of kids waiting to get off the bus, nodded his okay. Jug ticked our names for a clean get-away. After Bluey had been searched and sent to Dad-ak's office, Tyson went back to checking the roll until another Pigeon presented himself.

Everyone was satisfied with the end result. Tyson caught a few kids. That in turn made Dad-ak happy. Buyers got their herbs. The gangs that ran the operation got five per cent of the total purchase. After Bluey and the other Pigeons had been caned for their crime, they returned to their gangs, heroes.

'Mission accomplished,' Jug said, passing Bluey a packet of herbs for his trouble.

'Legs', the 'Chaff Cutter' and the 'flicks'

The night 'Legs' Blackwell first cranked up the Bell and Howell projector proved to be the beginning of a glorious era in our lives. As the flicker of light splashed onto the makeshift screen, it was like we were being transported out of the backwaters of time, into the modern 1950s.

By the following day the crystal sets we spent months building had become obsolete. The HMV wireless that attracted us like bees to a honey pot suddenly took on the shape of a monument to bygone days. The here and now belonged to the Bell and Howell; the 'Chaff Cutter' as it soon became known because of its habit of chopping film to pieces.

We took to the 'flicks' like ducks to water. Most were in black-and-white, with just the occasional one in colour. But black-and-white or colour, it didn't matter. When Legs turned on the Chaff Cutter, the hum-drum of everyday life was instantly forgotten. Even the pong from the nearby dairy, piggery, bull pen and poultry disappeared.

The flicks were held on Saturday night. Immediately after tea we grabbed our blankets and mosquito coils and congregated by the school hall. In winter we sat inside. In summer we stretched out on the lawn underneath the stars.

To open the feast of entertainment there was the Movietone or Cinesound Review newsreel. The problem of the news being a year out of date was irrelevant. Just the sight of the laughing kookaburra or the kangaroo hopping on the screen made us feel proud that we belonged to a world larger than our immediate environment. A point we were otherwise apt to forget.

Following the newsreel came the serials. These were discards from cinemas. We cheered the goodies with unbounded enthusiasm and booed the crooks with equal fervour. Toward the climax, when the crooks were creeping up behind the goodies, we shouted so loud that we just about lifted the roof off heaven.

'Watch out behind ya! The bloody crooks'll getcha!' Meat screamed above the racket. And it was just as well he did, because the goodies only heard him in the nick of time.

The serials arrived in a cruddy condition and rarely in any order. After the Chaff Cutter had done with them they were in shreds. Still, the bits and pieces we did see proved that there was no limit to the imagination of a script writer.

In 'Perils of the Wilderness' the cowboys lived with their horses at the end of Box Canyon in a huge cave hidden behind a rock, which was hidden behind a waterfall. When the police rang through the news of a crime, the cowboys turned a huge wheel inside their cave. The wheel turned the waterfall off and caused the rock to roll away from the entrance to the cave. The cowboys then galloped at full pelt from their cave, down the canyon track and onto the main road to chase and apprehend the car full of gangsters as they sped for the safety of the outer city limits.

Another favourite was 'The Shadow'. Just when the crooks were about to make good their escape, they were surprised by a biplane packed to the hilt with gun-toting cowboys.

'Kill 'em! They jus can't go 'round robbin' and shootin' innocent people like that, can they Jug?' Meat called.

Following the serials, while we tried to sort some sense out of what we'd seen, Legs set up for our next treat – cartoons.

For each of the cartoon characters we had our own special ritual. When Tweety appeared we yelled, 'I tawt I taw a puddy tat,' then scrimmaged around under our blankets in a mass mock search. With Bugs Bunny we turned to Doc Davis, scratched our heads and shouted, 'Ahhhh . . . what's up Doc?'

After the cartoons, chatter buzzed around the audience. When Legs set the spool, the main lights were turned off. The rattle and clatter of the Chaff Cutter echoed its warning. As the film count flashed on the screen, we chanted, 'FIVE! ... FOUR! ... THREE! ... TWO! ... ONE!'

Then the main feature hit the screen. And there we sat rapt for the next couple of hours – except during the breakdowns.

During a run of adventure films the school's bush rang with budding Tarzans. Meat pinched a length of rope from the tractor shed and strung it high in a river gum.

'That rope looks a bit worse fer wear, Meat,' Jug warned.

'Me Tarzan. Me tough. Me swing on anything in jungle,' Meat replied.

He stretched the rope back to its limit and pushed off. Down he swung in perfect pendulum motion.

'Ahhhhh . . .'

Then . . . SNAP!! The rope broke.

'Jug! . . . HELP!!' SPLAT!! Meat smacked headlong into a tree trunk.

By the time the season of adventure films had reached its end the student injury list stood at three broken noses, two broken arms, one broken leg, two concussion cases and bumps and bruises galore.

Legs then ordered in Westerns. We saw 'Stagecoach' and 'Red River' with John Wayne; some Audie Murphy films; Hopalong Cassidy; Roy Rogers and his faithful companion Trigger.

We called each other 'Pardner'. The lane between Mutch House and the laundry and Tuck Shop took on the look of the Wild West. Bodies were hurled from the downstairs Mutch House dorms, which had become the local bar-room and stud poker joint. Mock brawls broke out at the drop of a hat. At sunset the lane hosted a string of gunfights. The school oval was re-named 'Boot Hill', because that's where we buried our opponents.

Meat became an Indian chief. He painted his face and stuck galah feathers in his cricket cap. He roamed around saying 'How!' to everyone. He made a bow out of a gum sucker and fishing line. Wherever we went we were showered with arrows.

'Who the hell d'ya think ya are, Meat?' Jug snapped.

'Me Big Chief Sittin' Bull. Me lookin' for pale face to scalp.'

'Well I seen one just a couple'a minutes ago, over near Dad-ak's office.'

And Meat went off in search of a pale face, only to be captured by Dad-ak, who told him that he looked like an idiot and should start acting his age.

Following the westerns came the musicals, full of singing and dancing and other sissy stuff. Jug reckoned Legs was having a secret affair with Judy Garland and wanted to come back as Fred Astaire in his next life. But we never complained. If there was any Nit we didn't want to offend, it was Legs. It would have shattered us had he not turned up with his Bell and Howell on a Saturday night.

We suffered through Judy Garland in 'The Wizard of Oz' (three times), 'Easter Parade' and 'A Star is Born' (twice), plus all the Fred Astaire and Ginger Rogers films. And occasionally Meat burst into 'Somewhere Over the Rainbow' or snapped into a soft-shoe shuffle before realising his gaffe and withering in embarrassment.

Jug's and my favourite film idol was Humphrey Bogart. He was everything we aspired to be. During a term of high-sea adventures 'The African Queen' was shown. For weeks after, as did every gang, we were out bush building our own boat. By the end of term the stretch of the Murrumbidgee River from Horn Beach to Stag Beach was littered with as many sunken wrecks as was the Pacific during the Battle for the Coral Sea.

But if there was one film that we were busting to see, it was 'From Here to Eternity'. Horny's Dad had seen it in Sydney and he told Horny that it had one of the hottest sex scenes he'd ever seen.

'Please Sir, can ya get it? I'll try real hard in English. I promise Sir,' Meat pleaded.

And Legs didn't let us down. He worked out some deal with his film library contact and we got the film at normal cost plus a couple of boxes of mixed produce from our vegie garden and orchard.

The summer night that 'From Here to Eternity' was to be shown, our expectations were already sky high. And although most times high expectations fall short, we weren't let down. The film stunned us in many ways. But when Bert Lancaster and Deborah Kerr lay in a hot embrace with the foamy surf washing over them, our male hormones ran riot as never before.

'Gawd almighty Jug. Ain't she the prettiest thing you ever saw?' Meat sighed.

We begged Legs to rewind the reel so we could see the scene again. And I think he would have except he was afraid it might get back to Dad-ak and there'd be trouble. Still, my imagination had been ignited. For many nights after, I slept with my pillow in such an intimate hold that, as I drifted off to sleep, I could almost hear the hiss of the sea and smell the perfume on Deborah Kerr's skin.

A Rough and Ready Mob

On ANZAC Day, Jug's brother Joe arrived early for our small service. He sat under the trellis of roses next to the War Memorial, looking through his old scrapbook.

Joe never quite made it to the War. He'd tried to join the forces not long after becoming Yanco Ag's youngest bugler, but his parents wouldn't let him leave school. It was one of his greatest disappointments. But Joe's heart and soul were there, up on the front line with his school mates.

'It wuz at the beginnin'a '39, Swamp. The whiff'a war was in the air. That's when Yanco Ag's first Cadet Unit was formed,' Joe told me. 'So when war was declared we were ready fer the Huns. Down the front gate, an ol' corrugated iron dunny, "The Thunder Box", was our guard-house. Mornin' 'n afternoon drill was compulsory. We patrolled the river 'n around the school boundary.

'But bein' armed with nothin' but wood guns, pitch forks, hoes 'n shovels, we were mighty pleased that the Huns never made it down the river or ta the front gate.'

Joe reckoned that when the Governor-General passed through Leeton on a conscription drive, the Yanco Ag Cadets, along with the Leeton High School unit, formed the Guard of Honour. Joe had the picture in his old scrapbook. It came out of the local rag. He showed me. The picture was faded but Joe reckoned he was the one holding the bugle.

'The ol' Gov' took one look at us 'n said, "That mob look a bit rough 'n ready." 'N 'e was right on both counts. Rough we were 'n ready we were, as the Leeton mob found out durin' the all-in, after they started slingin' off 'bout what the Gov' had said. Still, who gives a stuff about looks. Anyway, it was that same rough and readiness that came through when the Yanco Ag Cadets went on ta join the forces.'

I hadn't realised just how many Old Yanconians had shaped the war until Joe told me. Apparently a couple were the last to leave Dunkirk. Quite a few fought in the desert, across Northern Africa. At least one – Joe 'Digger' Madeley – was in the Ninth Infantry, who held Rommel at bay as the 'Rats of Tobruk'. It was all there, documented in Joe's scrapbook. I saw it.

'See that bloke there, Swamp, the one with the bicycle over 'is shoulder, as ya can see 'e was one'a the first ont'a the beach at Normandy. "Spider" Murphy's 'is name; 'n Old Boy.'

Joe told me that lots fought along the Malayan Peninsula. They worked on the Burma railway. Some were POWs in Changi.

'Gen'ral MacArthur himself once said, "If we'd 'ad more like 'im, I'd'a returned a damn lot sooner'n this." Ya know who the great Gen'ral was talkin' about, Swamp? 'N Old Boy by the name'a Private "Wily" Whyte. No kiddin'. I 'ad 'is picture 'ere somewhere. Must'a lost it.'

Then there were the Old Yanconians who fought along the Kokoda Trail. There's a famous photograph where a Digger is helping a bandaged and blinded mate across a jungle stream. Joe had the picture in his scrap book, right there for all to see.

'See there, way in the back, Swamp. Ya gotta look close. But that bloke helpin' 'is wounded mate 'cross the creek, 'e's an Old Boy. In Third Year when I was in First 'e was. The name's "Killer" Ashford.'

None of these Old Yanconians became household names or great war heroes, but Joe said, 'They were tough as ol' boots. The stuff this country's made'a. Blokes who stood by a mate till the very end. Blokes who kept pluggin' on when everyone else 'ad chucked in the towel.'

And there were those who'd died. Joe rattled their names off: Goodhew, Dillon, Hinton, West, Meiklejohn, Milthorpe, McGrath, Lewis.

Joe had known most of them. He showed me their pictures.

He'd cut them out of his old school magazines and stuck them into his scrapbook.

''N the sad thing is, Swamp, none of 'em was much older 'n you when they died. All of 'em were mates like you 'n me little brotha. Ya prob'ly sit at the same desks as some of 'em; maybe sleep in the same beds.'

Sometimes it was hard to know if all Joe said was fair dinkum or not. He was the sort of bloke who thought that, if Jesus came back to earth, he'd come to Yanco Ag for his high school education. And what's more, Joe would make a fortune running the books on him doing a walk across the school lake.

Hollywood Bound

Meat McFadyen didn't get his nickname simply because his Dad was the butcher at Ungary.

Meat was a tall, lumbering, shy, pimply, awkward bloke who just happened to have an endowment that left the rest of us aghast with awe. What we believed we could do with just half of what Meat was born with defies description.

It was Jug who, upon sighting Meat in the Mutch House showers one day, was suddenly blinded by a spark of business inspiration. Jug came to the conclusion that, if Meat was managed astutely, he had the earning capacity to enable us to monopolise the school's black market trade in cigarettes, plus buy every copy of the keys to get into the kitchen, butter safe, meat safe, bread store and larder.

When Jug and I first approached Meat about the matter he didn't seem too keen on being used purely as a business undertaking. But during the discussions that followed, we discovered that beneath his shy exterior lay someone who flirted with aspirations of fame and glory.

It was on that tack that Jug decided to concentrate his vast management skills. Jug was determined that Meat wasn't going to become a one hit wonder. His 'new vision', as he called it, was of a far more sustaining nature. He began carefully to map out Meat's course toward fame and glory, as a boxing trainer would a prospective champion.

Jug reckoned that, after we'd cornered the local black market, his brother Joe had a few contacts who could swing a deal in the glamour world of Hollywood. There we'd break Meat into the lucrative blue movie scene.

''N with the profits,' Jug explained excitedly, 'you, me 'n Meat'll buy a mansion right next ta Errol Flynn. 'N we'll become mates 'cause we got so much in common. We'll have 'im over fer barbies 'n stuff, 'n drink champagne by the bucket 'n eat gallons'a ice cream. 'N the sheilas, Swampy. Joe reckons some'a them star types are real goers. 'N 'e should know. 'E's 'ad a few. He told me!'

Meat's first public appearance took place in the tractor shed before a huge crowd of fifty students. He was billed as the curtain raiser to another of Jug's promotions, the much awaited bout between Mark 'The Mangler' Mangelsdorf and 'Wild Dog' Dorkins. For an entry fee of two herbs per head, the audience watched Meat steal the show as he decimated 'Prick' Anderson's eight-year-old school record by hanging five wet towels over his erect penis.

The following week there was an inter-school football carnival over at Griffith. That's where Jug let the word escape about Meat's five-towel haul.

And escape it did.

The instant Meat got hold of the footy the opposition charged in from all directions to tackle him, inquisitive to find out if the rumours held any truth.

This situation placed Jug in a pickle: whether to bribe our Sports Master, 'Flash' Merino, to rest Meat on the reserve bench. While Meat was paramount in our future plans, Jug also had a bet going with Jack Hendersen from Leeton High that we'd take out the flag. And with the opposition concentrating so much on Meat, the pathways to their try line were left wide open.

Jug decided to let fate run its course. And thanks to Meat's much mauled distraction, we ended up beating Leeton High 18-12 in a torrid eight-stone-seven division Grand Final.

During the post-match celebrations Jug set Meat's next performance for our following term school dance.

'That's where Meat'll 'ave a go at smashin' the world record'a twelve wet towels,' Jug announced.

The month remaining until the dance worked in our favour. It enabled the news to filter through the other schools, and in particular into the female sector. The viewing price was set at one packet of cigarettes, and they had time to save, thieve, or otherwise acquire the cost of entry.

With double the normal number of girls turning up at the school dance, we were forced to change the venue for Meat's performance from the dressing room at the back of the school hall to the larger Farm Mechanics block. We spread the news of the change during the opening Progressive Barn Dance and set the time of the world record attempt for later in the evening, between the 'Pride of Erin' and 'Canadian Three Step'.

In case the Duty Nits thought that something untoward was happening, we made a special point of requesting that the girls make an inconspicuous exit from the school hall. But the moment the Clef Trio ground to a rasping halt at the end of the 'Pride of Erin', you could have sworn that someone had shouted, 'FIRE!'

A veritable evacuation took place. But luck was with us. When a group of girls were questioned about why they were leaving the hall in such a rush, one of them had the nous to blame it on the curried egg sandwiches they'd had for supper.

After leaving the hall, the girls ran around the back of the Farm Mechanics block. Jug had jemmied open the window and was on hand to hear the password – 'Hollywood Bound' – before receiving their entry fee. By the time Jug shut the window, we were sitting on the largest haul of herbs we'd ever seen.

To enhance the mood I lit a few candle stubs around the place and tuned the wireless into Saturday Night Requests on 2WG, the 'Voice of the Riverina'. Then, to the soulful sound of Bing Crosby crooning 'I'm Dreaming of a White Christmas', Meat drifted into the flickering light.

He'd dressed for the occasion in an old pair of oversized bib-and-brace overalls and gum boots, and began to stumble his way through a clumsy half-baked strip act he'd been working on for his Hollywood debut. The guarded giggles that this poorly performed routine brought turned into uproarious laughter when he tripped over himself while attempting to slip out of his gum boots. I feared that worse was to come. Then, as he was clambering awkwardly back onto his feet, Meat ripped off his overalls.

A huge gasp of shock spun around the Farm Mechanics block. The girls sat stunned. Jug entered from 'Tyson' Tynan's office. In his arms he carried the huge stack of dripping wet towels and started to excuse his way through the audience. When he finally reached Meat, Jug staggered under the weight of his load before placing it on a work bench. After pausing to catch his breath, Jug wiped the sweat from his brow, then began to drop each towel at the feet of our star attraction.

'ONE ... (Splat) ... TWO ... (Splat) ... THREE ... (Splat) ...'

With each solid, wetted slap of the towel the girls' jaws dropped lower. When Jug had finally jettisoned the thirteen towels, he bowed to the audience with an entrepreneurial flourish, thanked them for their attendance, and left Meat to do his bit.

Whether it was the proximity of the electric band saw, the chilly winter night or the shock of being faced by fifty goggling eyes, Meat couldn't rise to the occasion.

'Think about Marilyn Monroe!' Jug called out as a last resort.

But not even Marilyn Monroe could save Meat that night.

The spell had been broken and some disgruntled voices called for their cigarettes back. Jug, at the end of his tether, stormed to the fore. He snapped off the wireless, dumped the herbs on the work bench, blew out the candles and shouted, 'Sort out ya own bloody refunds.'

With a fortune having disappeared before our eyes, Jug and I sauntered back to the dance leaving Meat behind in the dark. The news had already reached the hall. Comments like 'What's the use of something that big if ya can't do anything with it?' only increased the devastation of our failed business venture.

To save face, Jug and I made our escape down to the piggery. There we shared our last remaining herb and rued the missed opportunity of high life in Hollywood.

'Ya know Swampy, I would'a really liked to've met Errol Flynn,' Jug sighed.

By the time we returned, the dance was thankfully over and the girls were filing back onto their buses to head homeward. As Jug and I were about to go back to our dorm, we heard noises from behind the Farm Mechanics block. Out from the shadows Meat appeared with a mob of girls. They were giggling and carrying on like they'd known each other all their lives.

Yet somehow Meat didn't quite look like the same bloke we'd left behind an hour or so earlier. That once slow, lumbering step and shy manner were now replaced by a glow of manly confidence. In true gentlemanly fashion he brushed the sawdust off each of the girls. Then, one by one, he swept them into his arms and gave them a lingering kiss, before they reluctantly staggered back onto their buses.

After Meat had completed his farewells we approached him.

'Ya can say goodbye ta Hollywood,' Jug sneered.

Meat seemed oblivious. He wandered out onto the middle of the road, not even noticing that he was being engulfed by a cloud of diesel fumes. He let out a long, animal growl then broke into an odd grin.

'Stuff Hollywood!'

Old Bandy

I wasn't a good student. I felt imprisoned in that double-storey class block, chained to my iron-framed desk, battling boredom and blotches of ink. The endless sirens wailed their warning of lessons to come.

The rest of our gang weren't much better. We all mucked around far too much.

'A bunch of bloody no-hopers,' Tyson Tynan once yelled over our rabble-rousing.

But those words struck us as more of a compliment than criticism. To us, what happened out on the sports field was of far greater importance than what happened in the classroom. Out there a bloke could become an instant hero by scoring a try or belting a century. Yet if he got straight 'A's, everyone kept their distance from him. They looked at him as if he was a stranger.

It became a vicious cycle. We started to fall behind in all subjects. And the more we fell behind, the more we mucked up. We rampaged through English, ripped through Science, raised hell in History, rejected Agriculture.

But Maths was different.

It wasn't that we were magnetically attracted to logarithms. Quite the opposite. It was just that old 'Bandy' Bains taught Maths. And Bandy was someone special.

While most of the other Nits were single and lived in the weatherboard teachers' quarters on the southern side of the school, Bandy, Rock-Jaw and Dad-ak were provided with houses on the property.

Like Dad-ak and Rock-Jaw, Bandy was married, though we never got to see his wife. There was a great mystery about that. Rumours abounded. Some said that Mrs Bains had ran off with a jackeroo from Willbriggie station; a bloke as bald as a badger, who couldn't count to ten. Others reckoned that she'd driven Bandy to the brink of insanity with her constant whingeing until, one night, she'd opened her gob once too often. She'd pushed Bandy that little bit too far. He'd snapped and murdered her, embalmed the body in wax, and laid it out in their bed. That way if anyone had entered the house they'd think she was in a deep sleep.

Most of the time it was best to believe only a fraction of what was said around the place. We leaned towards Jug's theory that Mrs Bains was a chronic invalid. So disabled, in fact, that she was unable to do the washing, mending, cleaning, or anything else. That forced Bandy and his son 'Young Bandy' into having to fend for themselves, which explained why Bandy never had to do the duties all the other Nits did, and also why he and Young Bandy always wore the same daggy clothes.

Young Bandy was a senior. He didn't board in a dormitory like the rest of us. He lived in the house with his Dad and his chronically-invalid Mum. Young Bandy was the strong, silent type. He hardly talked to anyone, let alone us, and that's why we never got the chance to find out the real truth about his mother.

Because Mrs Bains was unable to do the shopping, Young Bandy had ran out of underdaks. He used to walk with his penis flopping around inside his pants like a length of thick, uncoiled rope. Occasionally we'd follow him into the toilets just to get a gawk at it. But he always went into the dunny. He never used the trough like normal blokes did.

Then one day a horrific accident occurred. One that catapulted Young Bandy into the annals of Yanco Ag's folklore.

During a Monday morning Farm Mechanics lesson, Young Bandy was bragging about how strong he was.

'Ya full'a piss 'n wind,' his class mates scoffed.

Young Bandy saw an anvil lying on the work bench. To prove his mates wrong he lifted it off the bench, holding it high in the air. To get better leverage he leaned against the bench. This caused the front of his pants, plus its luggage, to inadvertently flop on top of the bench. On his third clean and jerk the anvil slipped. It plummeted back toward the work bench gathering speed at a rate of thirty-two feet per second squared.

SPLAT!! His 'old fella' was squashed between the anvil and the work bench. Hooly Dooley!!

If Young Bandy wasn't bandy like his Dad before the accident, he certainly was afterwards. Every time we saw him walking, we'd wince in pain with the thought of it. We couldn't even bring ourselves to try and get a gawk at the damage. We could imagine it. Young Bandy going for a pee, undoing his fly, and rolling it out like a length of carpet.

But if Young Bandy may have deserved what happened to him, old Bandy certainly didn't.

As Jug said, 'It was as good as signin' the old bugger's death warrant.'

Old Bandy had taught Maths at Yanco Ag for as long as anyone could remember. He'd even taught Jug's brother Joe back during the war, which was why Joe turned out to be so good at running the SP.

The thing was, Bandy didn't go about teaching the way the other Nits did. He didn't blow his top. He wouldn't go crook when we got something wrong. He never sent alarm bells off in our heads by clogging up the blackboard with equations that looked like a quagmire of worms. Bandy had the knack, that rare gift of knowing how to teach kids like us, and *always* had a helping word for those who were having the greatest difficulty.

He'd explain Pythagoras's Theorem as if it was an adventure story jam-packed with humour, fun, danger and excitement. One minute he'd have us laughing our heads off, the next we'd be clawing at our desks in trepidation. And, as he wove his tapestry of Maths around our retrograde group, he won us over. We forgot about mucking up. Our ears pricked as soon as he opened his mouth. We began to pay attention. Our fears abated and we began to think, 'Hey, this is pretty keen stuff.'

But just our rotten luck, the only teacher that we got along with and they had to give him the sack. Too old, they reckoned. Apparently he'd been cooking the books about his age for years, just so he could go on teaching ratbags like us.

What's more, the drama unfolded during one of our lessons. A letter arrived. As he read it he started to look real crook. That was unlike Bandy. He never had a sick day in his life. To him, teaching maths was a tonic far greater than any medicine a doctor could prescribe. It was the one thing that kept his heart pumping and the blood whizzing around his body.

We fell into inquisitive silence, wondering what drastic news the letter held. The longer we waited, the more we started thinking that perhaps we'd been wrong about Bandy. Maybe we were so dumb we couldn't see that his outer calm was just a front to cover up the inner turmoil of his murderous real self. Perhaps there'd been a tip-off and the police had broken into his house. They'd smashed down his front door with axes and sledgehammers, like they did in the flicks. When they'd barged into the bedroom, there she was, the embalmed Mrs Bains as stiff as a board in their marital bed.

Finally Bandy rose and called me outside.

'Why me, Sir?' I blurted, feeling the shudders of fear scuttling up and down my spine.

I followed him tentatively down the corridor and into the empty staff room. He handed me the letter and stood by the staff room window. I breathed a sigh of relief at seeing EDUCATION DEPARTMENT OF NEW SOUTH WALES.

But as I read on, things changed.

The letter had been written by some 'Joe Blow' from the big smoke. Someone who probably didn't even know where Yanco Ag was. Someone who wouldn't have known Bandy from a bar of soap; who lacked the vision to look beyond a person's name and birth date to find out what they were really like or how good they were at their job. They accused Bandy of cheating, lying about his age. His orders were blunt. He had to stop teaching when the term ended, in just two weeks.

After reading the letter I joined Bandy by the window. Together we stared out over the vacant quadrangle, me at a loss as to what to say, and he probably musing over the countless students who'd come and gone during his many years of teaching.

I heard him sniffle.

'You all right, Sir?' I asked hesitantly.

And old Bandy blew his nose and said, 'One of these days you'll make your mark on this world, son. It may only be a scratch, but you'll surprise a lot of people.'

In the Wake of 'Horny' Jones

As I stumbled through the grips of puberty, I struck a problem. Because there were no girls at Yanco Ag, I, along with the rest of my mates, spent my time gazing at girlie magazines. Those unreal images overtook my inbred passion for horses. They even overtook my lifetime love of cricket.

When it came to the crunch, however, the leap from fantasy to reality proved a real stumbling block. In the presence of a live female I felt awkward, shy and uncomfortable.

In the company of my mates, confidence reigned supreme. There I was amongst allies. I could make a quip that would render them helpless with laughter. I could hold them spellbound with my many tall stories, mostly about female conquests.

They were good stories too. And so they should have been. I usually spent most of my vacation making them up. There was the one about Bessie Smith over at the silos. Another about Bewler Saunders down by the Mirrool Creek. After a couple of holidays I'd run out of girls in Beckom. I invented some: Ingrid Goostaff, a Swedish beauty who just happened to stay at our house on her way to becoming a film star; Brenda La Volle, who doubled as Miss France; 'Hot Hips' Honey-Water, a trapeze artist from the travelling circus.

Yet, if truth be known, by my sixteenth birthday the total of my life's intimate moments consisted of eight French kisses. I'd also felt three breasts, two of them on the same girl; the one on the left-hand side and the one on the right.

I never told anyone that. It wasn't the manly thing to do, to admit being a virgin. It was easier to make something up. The more gross, verbose and descriptive the better.

I reckon that Jug had less of a clue about girls than I did. He told us once about how he and May Wilks had 'set the sparks flying' underneath the grandstand during the athletics carnival over at Wagga Wagga. That was a real humdinger.

'I tell ya fellers' – Jug summed the story up as if still exhausted from the experience – 'she was the hottest thing I ever knew. She could'a melted butter from ten yards away.'

What's more, we all believed him. That was until the news got back via a friend of a friend of May Wilks's that Jug had actually done his dash before they even had the chance to do anything.

Jug would never have lived that down. No bloke would. But I saved his bacon by telling the rest of our gang that it was a load of bull because I'd actually caught them.

'Saw 'em with my own two eyes, I did. Jug and May Wilks, goin' hammer and tongs at it.'

Actually I didn't go anywhere near the grandstand on the day of the athletics carnival. But Jug and I were best mates, and best mates always stick up for each other, no matter what. Anyway, we all probably exaggerated when all was said and done. All of us, that is, except Horny Jones.

If ever there was anyone I regarded with awe when it came to sex, it was Horny. He lived and breathed a certain aloofness that went with not being a virgin; like knowing that you were going to score a century every time you walked out on a cricket oval.

Girls were magnetically attracted to Horny. They described him as 'the one with the come-to-bed eyes'. And they must have meant it too. I'd seen girls walk all the way across a hall just to ask *him* for a dance.

Even in our first year, I remembered Horny telling us about the night he lost his virginity. Back then, most of us hadn't thought much about girls in a sexual way. Well, I hadn't anyway. But I wasn't the only one who sat agape as the mysteries of the female unfolded. By the time he'd finished we were like a catch of stunned mullets.

Then Bluey slowly raised his hand. 'Excuse me. Do ya reckon then that she might'a been one'a them contortionist types?'

Given the circumstances, I thought it was a pretty fair

question. One that could have shed a fair bit of light on some of the queries I had on the matter. But for some reason Horny laughed at Bluey. Then everyone else started laughing. So I joined in as well, though I really hadn't known why.

The following year Horny set another benchmark. He proved experienced well beyond his years when he decimated 'Barnacle' Bean's long standing 'Brassiere Undoing' record by three-and-a-half seconds.

Just before the Intermediate Certificate, he was catapulted into celebrity status after some girls from Leeton High were caught in a stolen car on their way out to school to see him. We'd have given our eye teeth to have been Horny then, especially when his name was mentioned in connection with the heist in the local rag.

All the ballyhoo surrounding that scandal only seemed to fuel Horny's reputation. He was mobbed at the next school dance. Jug and I assumed that, being Horny's mates, we'd score some luck by association. Yet on that same night neither of us could entice a girl outside the hall. Not even the ones that Horny had discarded in his wake; not even the 'wallflowers'.

As a last resort Jug turned to bribery.

'Look,' he said to a couple who'd been sitting down the back of the hall most of the night. 'Me 'n me mate Swampy'll chuck in a couple'a free cigarettes if youse come fer a walk outside.'

And they still wouldn't have a bar of us; not even the chain smoker!

Our Gang

During school holidays, I began to miss Yanco Ag. Like the rest of our gang I was a sports fanatic, and boarding school suited the outdoor types.

'Who's for cricket?' was all someone had to call and he'd be bowled over in the rush of volunteers. In five minutes flat there'd be two well equipped teams of 'Aussies' and 'Poms', eager to play the Test Match of their lives.

For the first week of holidays I couldn't work out why I had difficulty sleeping. I tossed and turned, tossed and turned. Then it dawned on me. The answer was the silence. I'd become used to the noise in a dorm full of kids.

With Dad being in the bank, I also missed the farm work. I had a dream about the dairy. It was lit by dull electric light. Before sunrise, sounds seem so intimate. In my drowsy state I heard the 'chug . . . chug' of the generator, the hiss and draw of the teat suction cups; milk whizzing around the observation bowls. My nose clogged with the rich aroma of creamy milk, slush, silage and detergent. There was the smell of the cows. The touch of their thick, leathery Jersey and Guernsey hides, rising and falling with each huge breath; the grinding of cud; the way the steam rose off the sloppy dung, dropped so nonchalantly. I lived through the remainder of that day with the same feeling of tiredness that had dogged me during my two week stint of having to rise at 5.30 am for dairy duty.

Down the lane from the dairy was the piggery, where the snorting, mud-caked Landrace sows jockeyed to be first at the kitchen slops and mash we threw into their food troughs. Above the greedy sounds of the sows gobbling down their food came the high-pitched squeals of the tiny, pink piglets being trampled in their enthusiasm to join the feeding frenzy.

There was the never-ending job of hosing and scrubbing out the sties. On winter mornings, when thick layers of ice covered the water troughs, if we grabbed a piece of piping it would freeze tight to our already aching fingers.

As the dry hot summer holidays lingered, I began to yearn for the comfort of irrigation, the sweet smell of freshly mown grass. There was the satisfaction of watching the channel water lick its way along the furrows that we spent hours digging, bringing life to the beans, onions, pumpkins and carrots we grew for school consumption.

With thoughts of food, my mind turned to the excited chatter of the school's dining room. Meals delivered on tray-mobiles by the kitchen maids. Mona, my fantasy.

'G'day Mona.'

'G'day darlin'.'

With those simple words, my mind ran riot and my legs turned to jelly.

The food was kept warm in stainless steel trays, bowls and pots. Fried eggs waxen with fat; lumpy porridge. The peanut butter was so thick that, after we eventually spread it on a slice of luke-warm toast, we coated it with a layer of honey or jam so it'd slide down our throats and not gum up our mouths.

Day in, day out, the menu never changed. Then, with our patience exhausted, we'd revolt. We'd stamp our feet and bang our knives and forks on the table until the dust rose from the floorboards and the dining room windows rattled. Cookie turned a deaf ear. To him, our hoo-ha didn't make a scrap of difference. The next day he'd dish up the same grub, as if he hated us.

Then, right out of the blue, a surprise! A gourmet special. A sponge cake, or 'sinker' as we called it. Or, if we hadn't pinched all the jam during a kitchen raid, a jam tart, thick and crusty. The Table Head nervously divided the sweets into seven exact serves. As we devoured the dessert, those grumbles and sick jokes about Cookie were forgotten.

'Gawd, this is heaven,' Meat said, licking his spoon as if it were a lollipop.

'You betcha,' I mumbled.

As the holidays passed, my home town of Beckom, once the centre of my universe, didn't seem the same. I was no longer the kid I'd been in primary school. My mates from those days were busy helping with the wheat harvest and I was forced to spend much of the time by myself. I'd become used to the company of hundreds of kids.

I even began to muse about Dad-ak and his rigid Sunday morning locker inspections. Jug and I would be up early to make dead certain we had everything neat and tidy. After breakfast we waited for Dad-ak's arrival.

'He's coming,' the whisper buzzed around the dorm.

At Dad-ak's entry, we snapped to attention at the end of our freshly-made beds. He'd get to me, give a scowl, and check to see if my bed was made correctly. Then he'd get to my locker. He'd run his finger along the shelves, searching for dust. He'd make sure that my clothes were neatly placed away; that my shoes and work boots were glistening.

He'd return to the end of my bed to give me the once-over, making sure that my hands were clean and my fingernails weren't grubby. Those of us who smoked had previously rubbed our fingers raw on concrete. Woe betide anyone who was found with a hint of nicotine stain. Dad-ak would turn to move on. I'd breathe a sigh of relief.

'Marsh!'

'Yes, Sir.'

'Get a hair-cut!'

'Yes, Sir.'

Then he'd see Jug.

'Ashton!'

'Yes, Sir.'

'Wipe that smirk of your face lad. You look like a bull frog.'

'Yes, Sir.'

Sunday evening we attended Church in the School Hall. We never looked forward to Church. Each week a minister of a different denomination came out to deliver the service. But it wasn't so much the sermons that we dreaded, it was what happened when the priest had gone. After the School Captain's address we left the hall, walking in single file past the Prefects. If they'd seen us up to any mischief during the week we'd be in for a strapping. Heaven help any kid that a cruel Prefect took a dislike to.

'Hey, you! I seen ya with ya shirt hangin' out!'
'When?'
'Does it matter when?'
'No.'
'Then get with the rest of ya mates over ta the Igloo!'

Still, there was the Monday morning assembly to look forward to. We'd gather at the front of McCaughey House to form into our house groups. With our House Captain at the fore, displaying the house flag, we'd march, LEFT, RIGHT, LEFT, RIGHT, down the Mutch House lane and around to the quadrangle, where we'd be called to stand at ease. House points were given for dress and marching.

Then came the announcements. When our names were mentioned for weekend sports achievements, everyone gave us a sideways smile and we brimmed with pride. If someone was cited for academic achievement, everyone 'poosed' at the offender.

Finally Dad-ak took the dais. No one moved when Dad-ak spoke; not a muscle. He gave a summary of the past and coming weeks, both the good and the bad. Mostly it was the bad.

'Some boys were seen out of bounds last Thursday afternoon.' As he cast his eye over the sea of faces before him, I knew he was looking directly into the depths of my guilty soul.

Tension filled the air when Dad-ak was around. Just to hear the jangle of his huge set of keys sent fear scuttling through my body. More often than not, his arrival meant that Jug and I were in trouble. But it was all the mischief and fun we put into making the trouble that kept our lives exciting. We both just about lived to test how far we could go before we got caught, caned and placed on detention.

As the days of my holidays came to a close I began to look forward to the sight of the thickly-wooded river gums out in the school's bush, the eucalypt heat, the crackle of dry leaves.

The Murrumbidgee River and its surrounds were as much our playground as were the sporting fields. The river was where most of us had mastered the dog-paddle and then other strokes. We dug trenches down the banks to make mud-slides into the water. Ropes were hung from overhanging branches so we could swing out like Tarzan before crash-landing in a belly-flop. Inflated tractor tyre tubes were used as rafts. We fished, potted for fresh-water crays, played beach cricket and football. There were strolls to Horn and Stag Beaches. We'd lie on the thin stretches of sand until the sun bit into our skin, then cool ourselves off in the murky waters, still chilly from the spring thaw in the distant Snowy Mountains.

The hair on the back of my neck rose when I thought about the kitchen raids. Hearts pounding as if we were spies going behind the Iron Curtain, we slipped silently into the kitchen to whack up a feast fit for a king. As a parting gesture we mixed salt into the sugar bowls at Rag's and Moof's table.

There were the dormitory raids. We spent hours plotting our attack before blitzing the 'enemy' with flour and water bombs, pillows blazing like six guns.

'Hit 'em hard. Hit 'em fast and bugger off quick,' Jug commanded, as if we were his crack troops.

Summer was the peak time. On a stinking hot night with a full moon, dorm raids went on left, right and centre. Not even our Dorm Prefects could stop us. We went crazy.

If we got caught we were sent to Rock-Jaw, the Deputy Head, for punishment. Some mornings the passageway outside his office was as packed as the Leeton saleyards.

'Backs to the wall, hands out, palms up,' he'd call, then march up and down giving the cuts.

Rock-Jaw was exhausted by the time he finished. He spent the day walking around with his right arm hanging limp. During one holiday he learnt to become ambidextrous so he could give the cane with both hands. After that he walked around with both arms hanging limp.

The thing I longed for most was to be back with Jug and the rest of my mates, Bluey, Meat and Slimy. 'Our Gang', as we called ourselves. We didn't need flash names like the other groups: 'The Silver Shadows', 'The Night Stalkers', 'The Moonlight Raiders'. That in itself made us different.

We'd first got together to build a hut out in the school's bush. Then one day Jug suggested a ritual to unite us as a proper gang. As Joe had done in his old gang, we stubbed a lit herb into our arms to form the circular scar of eternal brotherhood. The pain and smell of burning flesh were almost unbearable, but they brought a togetherness I'd never experienced.

From that day on, it was rarely 'I' who did something. It was more 'we' or 'our gang'. Just to talk to Mum and Dad about 'our gang' gave me the warmest of feelings; a feeling that, no matter how high the odds were stacked against us, if we stuck together, we'd win out in the end.

So anticipation welled inside me as I was taken back to school after those holidays. As Mum and Dad drove past Dad-ak's residence to pull up outside McCaughey House, my eyes darted about desperately in search of my mates.

I was off like a shot the instant I saw Bluey. I doubt if I even said goodbye to my parents. Bluey came running across the lawn to tell me that Jug had come back a day early and had convinced Rock-Jaw to reverse his parting comments and allow our gang to be in the same Mutch House dormitory.

'That bastard Jug could spin a bloody yarn around a trapdoor spider.' Bluey gasped at Jug's negotiating skills.

Bluey and I walked along the lane toward Mutch House, and the steamy humidity of the laundry hit me. The welcoming noise of kids swirled all around. I wasn't even put off by the sight of Rags and Moof skulking near the Tuck Shop, itching for a fight.

I sucked in the smell of the freshly varnished floorboards outside the dining room. My eyes rested easily on the rows of tables inside, covered as always in blue-and-white and red-and-white chequered table cloths.

'Ah, lamb spew for tea,' I said to Bluey as a joke.

At the bottom of the stairs, we instinctively flinched at the sound of Dad-ak's keys. We stepped aside to let him pass. Dad-ak took one look at me and said, 'So, you've returned to make my life hell again, have you?'

And just in that brief moment I thought I saw a faint smile beneath that gruff look. But I couldn't be sure.

'Yes Sir,' I replied, not in a smart way, but more out of a habit of obedience.

Bluey and I turned at the top of the stairs onto the Mutch House veranda, which overlooked the laundry and Tuck Shop. Then came the voice that I'd longed to hear.

'How the fuck-ar-ya, Swampy?' Jug yelled down the length of the corridor.

It suddenly struck me that swearing must have become fashionable over the holidays.

'Missed you, ya big shit!' I shouted back.

I dropped my suitcase and ran full pelt at Jug. He opened his arms wide to greet me. I threw myself at him. In one grab I had him in a headlock. With a quick twist and a flip I'd flung him flat on his back.

Ape

There was something weird about Ape; something dark, sinister and cruel. It even showed in his features. He had long black whiskers growing out of his cheeks. Beady eyes, as black as sin. He was shapeless.

Each and every one of us lived in fear of Ape, armed as he was with a cane he'd brought back from a merino feasibility tour of Borneo. No one dared challenge him. When Ape let rip, kids a hundred yards away clenched their hands as if to hold back the imminent blood-blisters.

Meat's experience of the cuts from Ape was, at first, no different from what happened to all of us at one time or another. It started when Meat, along with the rest of our class, handed in his Weed Collection Assignment a month before it was due.

To be punished for handing in an early assignment may seem odd, but there's more to it than that.

Weed Collections had a long history at Yanco Ag. The school's first Headmaster, Ernest Breakwell, had worked with the Department of Agriculture before becoming a teacher. As an eminent botanist, he became widely known in the field of grasses and weeds. So when the school opened, the first project in Agriculture was to get a Weed Collection together.

The enthusiasm for what had once been the most sacred of projects waned as the years rolled by. By the time our turn came, it had become almost the norm for the younger kids to buy their weed collections from the seniors. Some collections had been passed down through the generations until the kumbungi was like bleached straw and the paspalum seed resembled pepper. Still, a collection in good nick, which may have picked up a few distinctions along the way, was considered a treasure and could be worth as much as five packets of herbs on the market.

Once we'd bought our collection, we'd cut out the weeds, stick them neatly on a new page then copy down the relevant information to make it look as if it had been our own work. This saved lots of time and energy that we students thought could be far better spent on more absorbing agricultural topics like reproductive systems.

When Ape strode into class and saw the assignments neatly placed on his desk, he immediately called, 'How many of you miserable lot have purchased your Weed Collections from the seniors?' Surprising even himself, Meat stuck his hand in the air and owned up. Before he had a chance to realise his gaffe, Ape was dragging him off to the staff room for a caning.

If Ape had simply left it there, I reckon Meat wouldn't have done what he did. It would have all been forgotten. But Ape didn't leave it. For some reason he decided to take it further.

Another of Ape's responsibilities was to organise the Stock Duty Roster. The following week, Meat found himself on Dairy Stock, with the humiliating First Year's job of rising before sunrise to round up the cows for milking.

Meat was a wreck after a month's straight dairy duty. After two months he was a walking zombie. Then one night when Ape was supervising our nightly Prep, Meat fell asleep at his desk.

'I'll give you something to keep you awake, McFadyen,' Ape shouted.

Meat was taken off to the staff room and given the cuts. When he returned his tired look had turned strange. He lumbered back to his desk, sat down, laid his head in his arms and pretended to snore as loudly as possible.

Ape was at the classroom door in a flash, ordering Meat back to the staff room. Meat seemed almost eager as he walked off for the second time. We sat at our desks bewildered, flinching each time the cane ripped into his hands.

No sooner had Meat returned than he started up his mock snoring again. After a short burst he shouted out at the top of his voice, 'I'm still fallin' asleep, Sir. Have ya got somethin' stronger ta keep me awake?'

Ape took up the challenge.

Again and again, Meat taunted Ape into caning him. All the kids in school block soon cottoned on to what was happening. Even the downstairs classrooms fell silent as they listened to Meat pitting himself against Ape.

Meat's hands were a mess after five canings. But it was like he'd been possessed by some strange force. Meat wouldn't give in. Nor would Ape.

Our supervising Prefect, Huggy Holdsworth, tried to talk some sense into Meat, but he wouldn't have a bar of it. Then Jug had a go at him. 'Fer Christ's sake, Meat,' Jug pleaded. ''E'll kill ya.'

We all feared that there was more than a hint of truth in Jug's words.

Meat didn't even listen. He sat at his desk like a madman, his eyes rock hard. He worked himself up into a frenzy until he was panting like a dog. Then he leapt up for another dose of the cuts. Jug and I tried to hold him back, but he turned on us.

'Someone's gotta teach him, Jug!' he spat, then shoved us out of the way to go to the staff room, where Ape was waiting.

That was Meat's last visit. We sat helpless, hoping in vain for a miracle as Ape's cane rang out like a stock whip gone crazy. Then, on the second set of six, it happened. The cane splintered into shreds.

Ape sounds sprang up like in a jungle. The chant spread from classroom to classroom. Someone started stamping feet. We all joined in. The ape noises mingled with the thunder of pounding shoes. Books were hurled. Desk lids crashed open and shut.

Meat appeared at our classroom door amid the gathering riot. He lifted his hands high for all to see and called out above the uproar: 'I done him fair and square, Jug. I done Ape at 'is own game.'

The Once-a-Term School Dance

The once-a-term school dance was the most eagerly awaited event on our calender. On that night we renewed contact with the wonders of the female.

For months before we'd dream that this would be the moment when an Ingrid Bergman, or one of the scantily-clad women from Horny's collection of girlie magazines, would fall passionately in love with us.

Jug took up his scissors and bowl to charge three herbs for a basin cut. 'Doc' Davis concocted all sorts of treatments for pimples – 'krits' as we called them – plus any other ailment that he thought may hamper us in our quest. Horny conducted lessons on the correct way to approach a woman, and on romantic dialogue.

'Jus' remember,' Horny advised Jug, me, Meat and Bluey, 'girls are human, jus' like you 'n me.'

And by the way Jug smirked I knew what he was thinking, because I was thinking the exact same thing.

The Dance Committee spent the week preparing the school hall. They washed the walls, and scrubbed and mopped the floor. They fixed the seats and set them around the perimeter of the hall. The piano was rolled out and dusted, and 'Sharp Ears' Shea came from Leeton to give it a tuning.

'The old bugger could tune fencin' wire if 'e wanted ta,' Jug marvelled.

On the day of the dance, crepe paper, streamers and balloons were hung from every vantage point. Being an agricultural school, the odd gum branch, hay bale and show ribbon appeared. To add to the atmosphere, coloured cellophane was wrapped around every second light. As a final touch, sawdust was sprinkled over the floor to provide the smooth gliding surface that two left feet required.

The boiler exhausted itself on dance night as we washed ourselves squeaky clean. Faces were scrubbed red raw just in case Doc had overlooked soap as the miracle cure for acne. We shaved off our invisible whiskers, and ironed our shirts, ties, socks and even our underpants, just in case. Our best school trousers were taken out from between the mattress and the bed base where they'd been pressed for the past month. We plied our hair with gallons of Brylcreem or heavily-scented Californian Poppy. Our faces stung with Old Spice aftershave.

'This is gonna be my night, Swampy,' Meat announced.

When we'd readied ourselves, we passed our time sitting around the dorm reshining our shoes in the hope that they'd act as a mirror and we'd dance with a girl who'd forgotten to put on underwear.

Gazing down onto the toes of our shoes while attempting to dance never helped our already crook technique, and having to wear black shoes made our quest an impossibility. Though Jug once told Rags and his mates that he'd just danced with a girl from Griffith and had seen 'all the way up'. That lie caused a brawl to break out amongst Rags's gang over who was going to have the next dance with the unsuspecting girl.

After tea, as if drawn by some mystical power, we slowly congregated on the lawn outside the school hall. Those sensing the heightening tension crept around the back, into the toilets for a smoke. We felt more manly with a herb in our hands.

'I tell ya, Swampy,' Meat said, blowing a smoke ring. 'Tonight's me lucky night. Can feel it in me bones, I can.'

Then, as he finished the remainder of his herb with one mammoth drag, the news flashed around that the band had arrived. There was always talk about hiring one of the emerging rock-and-roll bands, but it never came to anything. It was imperative that the evening went as smoothly as possible. There was too much at stake to gamble on the unpredictabilities of rock-and-roll.

Our regular band was The Clef Trio, a tight little unit led by 'Gran' Smith on piano. Backing Gran was 'Pop' Smith, who played the saxophone and swapped to an oboe on the rare occasion he wanted to change the feel of the music. The third member of the trio was Gran and Pop Smith's daughter Julie, who played the drums.

Jug reckoned that in her day Julie had been a Miss Leeton Show Girl. Then with the world at her feet something went hay-wire. The pressures of pending fame and fortune proved too much.

'She took ta the bottle she did,' Jug explained. 'Lost 'er marbles 'n turned randy. Had more blokes than breakfasts she has. One of 'em was a bloke from Yanco Ag. "Jangles" Griffin was 'is name. Not that long ago neither.'

Julie looked quite normal at the start of proceedings. But, aided by the flagon of brown muscat she kept hidden behind the bass drum, toward the end of the evening her reckless soul returned with a vengeance. Her eyes took on a look like she'd been possessed by evil spirits. She'd let loose and thrash the drum kit to within an inch of its life.

As I sat watching her set up, she looked so frail and sedate, almost angelic. In my lonelier moments I tried to imagine myself as Jangles Griffin, having a torrid affair with Julie.

Suddenly my thoughts were interrupted.

'There's a bus coming!' someone yelled.

I forgot about Julie and ran out the side doors to the lawn. The moment of truth was about to arrive. This was where my idle dreams and boastful talk had to be turned into action.

We boys kept far enough away from the bus so as not to appear over-eager, but close enough to see the girls. We watched as they paraded in single file out of the bus and in through the main door to take up their seats along the far wall. There they sat, staring at us gawking back at them as if they were aliens.

'She's not bad, that one under the window. The one with the black hair,' Bluey said.

'Nah,' said Jug, the voice of experience. 'That one in the pink's better. Reckon she'd be a real goer.'

'Well I like the one in red,' Meat sighed. 'She's real pretty.'

'Nah. You wouldn't know if your arse was on fire, Meat.' The voice of experience, again.

By the time the buses from Leeton, Griffith and Narrandera High Schools had dropped off all the girls, we'd picked our most favoured one. Then, just in case anything untoward happened, we also picked our second, third, fourth and fifth choices.

As usual the first dance of the night was the Progressive Barn Dance. Being progressive, it was our big chance to inspect each of the girls we'd chosen from a distance. The problem was that there were far more boys than girls and we had to be quick to grab a partner.

The instant Gran Smith stood to announce the dance, Horny's lessons about the correct way to approach a woman went completely out the window. It became dog-eat-dog as we stampeded across the hall. Friendships were forgotten. Meat elbowed Jug out of the way. Jug elbowed me. Bluey fell over in the rush. We latched onto the first girl we came across and virtually dragged her onto the dance floor.

Seemingly oblivious to the melée below them, the Clef Trio burst into music. We were left in their wake attempting to organise ourselves. Then, when the dance finally got under way, I bided my time until the girl I was keen on was catapulted into my arms. The first thing I did was to give her a discreet checking over. When she looked okay on that closer scrutiny, I attempted to strike up some sort of conversation.

'What's ya name?' I asked. To see if she was agriculturally inclined like me, I tossed her a real curly one: 'Reckon it'll rain?'

At the end of the Progressive Barn Dance the girls retreated to their side of the hall, us boys to ours. An in-depth discussion on the finer points of women followed.

'She looks pretty good but she's got smelly ol' baby-powder on.'

'Well, the one I like, she wears perfume!'
'Which one's that?'
'Not sayin'.'

Perfume was the key. If a girl wore perfume it was obvious that she was the worldly type. Lipstick and nail polish were banned in schools and worn only by the more hot-blooded rebellious types. If a bloke latched onto a girl who looked vaguely like Ingrid Bergman and wore perfume, lipstick and nail polish, we reckoned he was in for the night of his life.

As Julie began to get into some sort of rhythm on her drums, the night progressed onto the more difficult dances. Here my romantic aspirations struck a snag. Out of our gang, Horny was the only one who knew how to dance. While he criss-crossed the floor as if floating on air, I stumbled about apologetically.

'Ouch! Yer trod on me foot, yer bloody horse!'
'Sorry. Someone shoved me.'
'Can't yer dance?'
'Course I can. I've just forgotten what this one is.'
'It's the Fox Trot.'
'Oh, I thought Gran said it was somethin' else.'
'What'cha deaf too?'
'Pardon?'

To make dancing even more difficult, desperation had drawn the blokes without partners in through the side doors from the outside lawn and out onto the dance floor.

'Thanks for the dance.'
'Thanks fer the broken foot.'
'Sorry.'

During dance breaks spasmodic conversation broke out between the more confident blokes and the girls. If Jug and I hadn't found a partner, we'd stick close by on the off-chance of being drawn into the conversation.

Around mid-evening, the trellis tables were set up in front of the stage and supper arrived on massive wooden trays. The food selection always consisted of white bread sandwiches: lamb and chutney, chicken and lettuce, beef and pickle, and curried egg. There were also fruit cake, assorted biscuits and lamingtons, and an urn bubbled away on the stage to fill pots for steaming hot tea.

Supper was more than the chance to fill an empty stomach. It was also a time to gauge the situation.

'Want'a share a plate of grub?' I'd ask my partner in my deepest voice.

If the answer was yes, it meant that she was happy in my company. I'd grab a swag of food and we'd sit together munching away while I tried to think of something to talk about.

If I was having a disastrous night, it was time to sneak out of the hall and gather some Dutch courage by having a quick puff and a swig of the potent 'Jug's Jungle Juice'. If someone had given up all hope, he'd console himself by scoffing down the untouched tray of curried egg sandwiches that'd been left by those who didn't want the remainder of their night spoiled by bad wind.

'Gawd almighty, Swampy,' Meat lamented. 'Jus' 'cause a bloke don't look like a film star don't mean she can tell ya ta bugger off like that. All I asked fer was a bit of a pash.'

'But that was durin' the progressive barn dance,' I told him. 'Remember what Horny said. You have to give 'em a bit of time to get to know ya.'

The second half of the evening was spent wondering how my partner might react to the offer of a walk down behind the bull pen. It was automatically understood that the girls knew what a visit to the bull pen was all about. If they weren't, and accepted the invitation, they'd be in for one hell of a shock. It was no small wonder that Brutus, the school's prize stud Hereford bull, was always in a foul mood after a night of listening to what went on behind his pen.

As we shuffled about, I'd dig deeply into my reserves of courage to blurt, 'H-h-how about . . .' Then I'd freeze.

'What were you gonna say?' she'd ask.

'Oh, nothin',' I'd reply in a coy sort of way.

'You were.'

'I wasn't.'
'You were!'

Then we'd fall back into silence, that barrier of communication now broken. If she allowed, I'd hold her a little tighter, close my eyes and breathe in the dizzy smell of perfume. And as we slid about I'd have a raging argument inside my head about what a gutless wonder I was.

Everyone congregated for the final waltz. Even if by some rare chance there was a girl who hadn't managed a dance all night, she was assured of at least twenty last-minute suitors.

Some of the hall lights were turned off and Julie crashed, banged and walloped into her crazed waltz drum solo.

But I was no longer interested in the music. I knew that, for me, there'd be no tomorrows, and after that Slow Waltz I'd probably have to wait for a whole term to find myself once more in the arms of a girl. As Julie brought The Clef Trio in to crash land, I'd attempt to steal a kiss before the girls, worn ragged from a night of enthusiasm and clumsiness, limped back to their buses.

Then they were gone. And more often than not I never saw the same again. Their co-educational schooling presented temptations that my mates and I never had the opportunity to enjoy.

On the rare occasion a girl wished to keep in contact, she'd send scented love letters to which I'd over-keenly reply. Or somehow she'd manage to smuggle out the leftover cakes and biscuits from her Home Economics lessons.

Still, I never gave up hope that at the next once-a-term school dance, a fabulous twist of fate would occur and I'd end up in the arms of the girl of my dreams. Until then, I remained with my visions of Ingrid Bergman and the sweet scent of perfume that lingered on my school blazer.

A Night at the Oscars

Attending an all-male agricultural boarding school wasn't the greatest of launching pads into the world of 'the Arts'.

To me, painting meant being handed a six-inch brush, a couple of gallons of paint, and being ordered to do a good job on a shed. Dancing was for sissies. The school choir struggled because our voices kept changing. And, coming from a small bush town where anything over ten people was considered a crowd, the thought of having to stand up and perform in front of an audience was daunting to say the least.

To put some balance into our lives, Dad-ak instigated an annual Play Night. In an attempt to get as many parents and relatives as possible to come along, it was held in the middle of winter, the slow time on the family farm.

Ma Dad-ak tried her best to add something special to the evening by inviting a handful of 'Guests of Honour'. These usually turned out to be people that she would like to have rubbed shoulders with, had her husband been a Headmaster of a posh city boarding school where money and the arts went hand in hand.

To give us every opportunity to impress these Guests of Honour with our one-act plays, Dad-ak allotted rehearsal time of a school period per day for almost a term.

A Nit was assigned to each class to teach us the basics, no matter whether they had acted before or not. Most of them hadn't. Invariably the burden was placed squarely on Legs Blackwell and Thomp Thornton to share the duties of Director/Producer/Stage Manager/Voice Coach, plus whatever else was needed to guide us through the rigorous rehearsals.

Day after day we'd go over our play until we could almost do it in our sleep. And yet, after all those hours, it was amazing how the words vanished from my mind the instant I squinted out through the stage lights to a real audience.

Those of us who remembered all their lines proved to be the exception rather than the rule. Our one-act extravaganza was tossed into disarray by the pressure of performance. 'Ad lib!' became the order of the day as the play's plot suddenly shifted from a murder mystery drama into a mysterious melodrama.

Some kids froze completely. Others stuttered like machine guns. Most mumbled so quietly that even their fellow actors had to strain to hear what they were saying. And there were those who were so occupied with throwing up in the outside toilets that they never even set foot on the stage.

But if Legs and Thomp ever drummed one golden rule about acting into us, it was 'The show must go on'.

So it did. And amid the mayhem, with blokes dressed up as females and all the real blokes having to proclaim their manhood by gluing false moustaches to their top lips, I remained ever-thankful that the entire cast always tried to learn every single line in the play.

The theory behind this was that we'd never get caught napping when our turn came to say something. It also rid us of the need for prompts or understudies. When an actor forgot his lines, the cast were right on hand to bale him out. We'd gather around and have a chat about the problem, then be straight back into it, almost as if nothing had gone wrong. Learning every line also helped when you had to take on dual roles after one of the actors was waylaid outside or was suddenly overcome with stage fright and turned into a statue with wetted pants.

This technique saved us all from time to time, but we often heard how we looked like a tank of goldfish on stage, silently mouthing each other's lines.

An adjudicator was appointed for Play Night. He or she was a prominent citizen in the community, involved with the Repertory Theatre: a doctor or a vet, or the wife of the local Member of Parliament, who'd acted in 'Arsenic and Old Lace' or some other classic during its three-night sell-out season in the Leeton Presbyterian Hall.

To get a closer view of the spectacle and have a better chance of hearing what was going on, the adjudicator sat at a large wooden desk near the stage, in front of the Guests of Honour. It was the adjudicator's job to award points to each play and its actors, culminating in presentations at the end of the night.

Awards were in two categories, Junior and Senior, and were given for Best Play, Best Supporting Actor, Best Drama, Best Comedy, and, of course, the ultimate, Best Actor.

The actual presentations took as long as two one-act plays. We didn't mind. With so many prizes up for grabs, most of us won something or other.

Beyond the bedlam on and off the stage there was always something magical about Play Nights. The Memorial Hall took on a totally different atmosphere; almost like I imagined a real theatre to be. And, as I stumbled through my part, I got a sense of how the great actors must have felt.

There was the excitement that swept up from the audience, spurring me on to greater heights. I experienced the feeling of being juiced up on raw nervous energy. There was the smell of cold cream and make-up; the deathly silence that pervaded the hall when the play moved toward its dramatic climax; the pure pleasure of bringing laughter to people.

Plus there was the applause. And it was loud.

Three hundred people clapping in a packed hall made one hell of a thunderous racket. And although the appreciation probably came from the audience's relief that we'd somehow managed to survive the experience, it didn't matter. Just to hear that applause made me feel like an Oscar winner. At its sound, the rigid knot of nerves which had been tightening in my stomach for months was suddenly released. It flooded my entire body, sticking in my Adam's apple, choking me with emotion, and making my eyes go watery. My mind came aglow with a giant neon sign flashing the words:

THIS IS BETTER THAN DRIVING A TRACTOR!

There I'd stand, beaming from ear to ear. Lapping it up for all the world to see, while silently wishing for the curtains to get stuck open so the audience would feel obliged to continue clapping.

Even when I went to bed, I was still riding high on that carpet of applause. So much so that I'd dream about being a famous actor. Someone who wasn't awkward, or gangly, or ravaged by acne. Someone who was confident in life and lived in a Hollywood mansion with ten gorgeous women, all with larger breasts than the Osborne twins from Narrandera. And every time I stepped out on stage the audience burst into such spontaneous and prolonged applause that the writers and directors only gave me a couple of lines to learn or else, with all the interruptions, their play would never reach its end.

But Yanco Agricultural High School had a funny way of putting things into their proper perspective. That line between dreams and reality was well-defined. At sunrise the next morning I'd stagger out of bed, rain, hail or shine, and go to work on the school farm; milking the cows, feeding the pigs, weeding the vegetable gardens. And all those glorious sounds of halls brimming with applause soon faded into a distant echo.

The Twenty Per Cent Factor

Who'd want to be a School Prefect? All those responsibilities: acting as one of Dad-ak's disciples; upholding the school's principles; nursing a dorm of snotty-nosed kids; supervising a classroom of ratbags during their nightly Prep; being a Table Head trying to control six rampaging vultures.

Who'd want to be a School Prefect? We all did! And why? Because it got the girls in!

A survey conducted during Joe's time showed that a female was 20 per cent more likely to accept an offer to go out with a School Prefect than a non-prefect. Now we weren't any great shakes at maths, but a blind man could see the advantages.

Due to a rural crisis, quite a few kids in our year went back onto their family farms after the Intermediate Certificate Exams. Out of our original gang, however, only Wiz Watson had left. He'd gone into the priesthood. Still, by Fifth Year, and even with our numbers so low, I wasn't confident of becoming a Prefect.

'Ya been born with rotten luck, mate,' Jug once told me. 'The sort'a rotten luck that gets ya caught most'a the time.'

The election for Prefects was held in the first weeks of the year. Every student had to vote. With most of our gang being reasonably popular, our election should have been assured. But there was one huge obstacle in the way – Dad-ak, who had the power of veto over anyone he thought was unfit.

On the Sunday after elections Dad-ak notified the blokes who were to become Prefects. As the day dragged on and I hadn't been summonsed to his office, things looked grim. By mid-afternoon everyone in our gang, except Slimy and I, had been told. Then, late in the afternoon, Dad-ak took the unprecedented step of appointing a couple of Fourth Years as Prefects.

After tea I was down in the dumps, so I went around the back of the laundry to have a herb in the tennis shed. I was contentedly puffing away when Tyson Tynan appeared at the window.

'You,' he snapped. 'Report to the Head immediately!'

It came as quite a shock when I arrived in Dad-ak's office fully expecting to be punished for smoking and was told I was going to be a Prefect. Although, as Dad-ak clearly pointed out, it was only due to lack of numbers, and even then it'd been a toss up between Slimy and myself.

I was over the moon.

My Mum was also over the moon. Not for the same reason. She didn't know about the 20 per cent factor. Nor did I mention how I was only becoming a Prefect more or less by default. But poor Mum got it into her head that I'd accomplished one of life's great behavioural turnarounds, something akin to the devil suddenly becoming religious.

Although my parents had moved to a little place in the north-east of New South Wales during my Fourth Year, there was no way that Mum was going to miss out on my investiture. She got Dad organised and they started out on their four day journey.

By the time they arrived, Mum was a nervous wreck. Dad said she'd been having a recurring nightmare that I got expelled just as I was about to be called up on stage to take the Prefect's Oath.

The fear that the nightmare would come true wasn't aided by the drawn-out proceedings on the day. It was as hot as Hades. The school hall was like an oven. Sweat poured off us all. When Dad-ak took the podium he went into waffling mode. On and on he went about how being a Prefect wasn't only a position of the highest honour, but also gave us a competitive edge when we ventured into the outside world.

'Being a Prefect at Yanco Agricultural High School gives a student a 10 per cent better chance in life,' Dad-ak announced.

'And a 20 per cent better chance with the girls,' Meat mumbled.

As an example of one of the school's great achievers, Dad-ak cited our honoured guest, Sam Longstaff. 'Loop-hole', as he'd been nicknamed, had apparently always shown a bit of a flair with figures. Joe had told Jug how Loop-hole had the makings of a world famous chef, the way he could 'cook the books'.

After leaving Yanco Ag, Loop-hole had completed a correspondence course in accountancy before going on to become the President of Batlow Apple Growers' Co-operative. When the Co-op had gone bust during the depression, he somehow snared a job in the Treasury. It was there that he had risen to great heights.

Loop-hole said how important it was to face our responsibilities in life. And the first real responsibility he'd faced had been as a School Prefect. To finish off, Loop-hole led us through a minute's silence for all the Old Yanconian's who'd fallen during the Second World War.

Our moment had finally arrived. We were called on stage in alphabetical order to receive our badge and take the oath.

With the nightmare still fresh in her mind, Mum had already been hanging off the edge of her seat. Then, with her fears skyrocketing, those final minutes to get to 'M' in the alphabet must have felt like a millennium.

It all proved too much.

The instant my name was called, all those years of pent-up parental stress, tension, disappointment, and at times downright depression, were suddenly released. Mum snapped. She leapt out of her seat and shouted down the hall, 'That's my son. That's my son!' Then she collapsed into sobs that continued, much to my embarrassment, throughout the remainder of the ceremony.

'Lucky ya weren't School Captain. Ya Mum might'a had a heart attack,' Jug quipped afterwards.

Somehow Jug swung it so that the dorms we were to look after were in upstairs Mutch House. Both of us had a group of Second Years.

The first thing that every Prefect did was to erect himself a 'dagging hole', which was a small study den made by rearranging lockers around your bed and desk and covering the entrance with a grey school blanket. This gave us a little more privacy, and shielded the others from the light of the midnight oil that we were supposed to be burning.

Our particular dagging holes were set in a line of four along the enclosed veranda at the southern end of Mutch House. There were Bluey, Meat and I, with Jug at the far end. Jug had the advantage. Being at the end, it took that little bit longer for an invading Nit to reach, allowing extra time to stub out a herb or whatever. Jug's dagging hole also proved the ideal place to run the SP and to conduct dusk-to-dawn card sessions.

So, we'd reached Fifth Year: our final year. The pinnacle of life. Other than our Prefect's duties, Fifth Year shaped up as a time of freedom – as far as freedom goes at a boarding school. With the privileges we'd tallied up over the years we could now stand at the front of any line, order kids about like they were servants, roll the cuffs of our shorts up three times. Our lockers weren't inspected on Sunday mornings. We were exempted from Stock Duty and didn't have to go to bed at any set time.

As Dad-ak said, we'd 'come to the age of responsibility' and now it was up to us to put in the huge effort needed to pass our final year examination tests.

Who gave a hoot about examination tests? The only thing we were interested in was putting the 20 per cent factor to the test at the next term school dance.

The School Choir

During the first week of second term, a notice appeared.

> SCHOOL CHOIR PRACTICE
> TUESDAY NIGHT AFTER DINNER
> MEET AT THE BOTTOM OF THE DINING ROOM
> HURRY!
> EISTEDDFOD IN ONLY 8 WEEKS

As usual, Thomp Thornton was first there, sitting on the piano stool, at the ready, music opened expectantly at the dog-eared page headlined 'Greensleeves'. He was dressed to the nines in his neat pin-striped suit, shiny black patent leather shoes and a brand new tie. That tie was worn every day for the next eight weeks until after the Eisteddfod. His 'Choir Tie', he called it. He reckoned it brought luck.

Thomp's bulbous eyes rolled eagerly around in their sockets as wave after wave of boys poured out of the dining room. Down the Mutch House corridor they came, only to thunder right past him on their way to play footy or ping-pong, or to dash off in search of mischief.

It was a sad sight really. By the time the siren sounded for Prep, Thomp was still there, sitting with one boy by his side, a stray who'd got into a fight and could find no other safe haven from his tormentors.

All in all, it wasn't an auspicious beginning for the School Choir.

But it had always been the same. Thomp knew that. It was a tough task to get the choir going each year. If it had been an audition for a rock-n-roll band – something like Bill Haley and the Comets – it might have been different. But singing sweetly with perfect pronunciation and rounded vowels wasn't our bag.

This was footy season. A time where a bloke's true manhood came under the spotlight. A time of mud and muck and a good stoush behind the dressing sheds, not of dressing up in a school uniform to stand in neat rows and act like angels, while attempting to sing in three-part harmony.

The last sorts we wanted to model ourselves on were a bunch of choir singers. We modelled ourselves on real men. Men who took on a pack of forwards without flinching, who smoked, drank and swore like troopers. Those were our heroes, blokes who sang along with Slim Dusty on the wireless and set the sheep dogs wailing.

But Thomp was persistent. Deep down he knew that by week eight there'd be thirty kids, maybe more in a good year, waiting outside McCaughey House, ready to be taken to the Eisteddfod. He'd already booked the bus.

After waiting for a week, Thomp began the hard sell. During Prep he floated nonchalantly down the corridor past the classrooms. He peeked in through the windows to watch us slaving over our studies, and that skew-whiff smile of his would come to his face.

The following night he would appear again. Another smile. Yet this time he didn't pass. He entered the classroom and slowly walked up and down glancing at our work. Then, as he was about to step out the door, almost as an afterthought, he returned to the front of the class and stood by our Prep Prefect.

'Well boys,' he announced. 'What if I could organise choir practice to be held on Tuesday and Thursday nights during Prep?'

Suddenly the notion of being a member of the School Choir began to have more appeal. Those who had been toying with the idea of joining now saw some clear logic in it. Two hours of singing instead of two hours of homework seemed a fair trade-off; the lesser of two evils.

Then there were the others, the ardent smokers, the 'Herb Rats' as we called them. Thomp's suggestion also got them going. We were in week three and their herb stocks were already dwindling. After a quick mental calculation they figured out that by week eight, when the Eisteddfod was on, they'd be clean out. Then the pangs of nicotine withdrawal would be biting and their lungs screaming, 'If only you'd joined the choir and had the chance to sneak up town to buy a few packs, you wouldn't be going through this torture!'

A lot of thinking went on that night.

By the time the siren rang for Prep the following choir practice night, the back of the dining room was a sea of bodies. Amid it all was Thomp, strutting around, chest puffed out, eyes doing cartwheels. Before any of us had the chance to change our minds he organised us into a line and we filed past the piano attempting to sing along with whatever scale he played.

He called this 'grading'.

After singing the scale Thomp shouted, 'Soprano!' or, 'Tenor!' or, 'Bass!' – or, in the case of Meat, 'Back to Prep, McFadyen!'

Until the grading was completed we mulled around in our three groups discussing the more important things of life like footy. When all was done, Thomp called us to attention.

'Can anyone read music?' he asked.

This brought muffled laughs from our ranks. No bloke in his right mind would learn how to read music. That was girls' stuff. And if anyone did know, he wouldn't dare own up to it for fear of being stirred by everyone, including his mates.

As always, we began with 'Greensleeves'. Every year it was 'Greensleeves' and 'Over the Sea to Skye' which made up our repertoire. We just about knew them backwards. Perhaps that was our punishment for not knowing how to read music and being able to tackle something different within the limited time remaining until the Eisteddfod.

When we first began singing, the noises we made reminded me of the Farmall tractor being cranked on a frosty winter morning. And as we continued to practise, week in, week out, things didn't improve much because there was another problem continually putting a spanner in our choral works: puberty.

The majority of the choir was going through that difficult stage of life. A bloke could be a soprano at one practice and by the next he could have plummeted to a tenor or even to a bass. Sometimes it worked the other way about. But that was puberty. Anything could happen, and it did, just when you least expected it.

This forced Thomp to forever reshuffle us. But never once did he give up. Thomp lived for that choir. And as I stood there miming among the toneless, ragged and raspy voices, I wondered if Thomp's enthusiasm may have overshadowed his ability to hear clearly. To me it was beyond comprehension how anyone could get so totally wrapped up with such downright crook singing. But he was. He pranced, gesticulated, rose to the tips of his toes with the high notes, sank to his knees with the low notes, weaved with the harmonies, shuddered at mistakes.

Finally the day of the Eisteddfod dawned. The bus rolled up and we clambered aboard, disgruntled and complaining about having to dress in our school uniforms.

'We look like a flock'a bloody canaries,' Jug grumbled.

The schools that entered the Eisteddfod were always the same. Other than us, there were Narrandera, Griffith, Wagga Wagga and Leeton High Schools. We were always at a disadvantage because the others had girls to prop up the higher end of the vocal scale, with softer, sweeter and more reliable tones than our mob.

We always came last in the competition.

'Fifth! Not last,' as Thomp would remind us on the bus trip back to school.

But on one particular day something beyond our wildest imaginations happened.

There was no breaking of voice, no bitter barking as someone's smoker's cough got the better of them. There were no shy efforts or laughs of embarrassment. As if it had somehow

Old Yanconian Daze

suddenly dawned upon us that there were no limits to this life. Our voices spun around Leeton Show Grounds Hall, echoing off the walls with such clarity that our bodies burst into goose pimples. I could feel it. It was electric. Everyone was pumped up, lifted, buzzing.

And so was Thomp. He stood in front of us conducting like he'd never conducted before. He hung for dear life on every note we sang; every minim, crotchet, quaver, every demi-semi-quaver. He rose so high with the high notes that he almost lifted off the ground. He sunk so low with the low notes that he almost skimmed the floorboards. He melded himself into our harmonies. And, as we came softly back to earth with the lowering of his hands, you would have sworn from the look on his face that he'd just brought an aircraft carrier into land right on the top of cloud nine.

We'd sung ourselves into second place.

She

I didn't see her file into the school hall for that last dance of my final year. She must have been hidden somewhere among the other girls from Leeton as they took up their customary positions along the far wall.

So I was caught by surprise when she slipped into my arms during the Progressive Barn Dance. Before I knew it, I'd blurted, 'Gee whiz, you look beaut.' While I was still flushing with embarrassment from my own outburst, she casually placed the palm of her hand to the back of my neck and replied how attracted she was to men who used Californian Poppy in their hair.

I couldn't let her go. When it came time to pirouette onto her next partner, I held onto her and the dance deteriorated into mass confusion. Amid the shamble on the dusty floor, with everyone calling at us, I made an unprecedented move. I told the rest of the dancers to 'bugger off' and leave us alone because we'd already decided to be partners for the night.

And when the dance continued, she was still there, right by my side. She looked up at me with those huge brown sparkling eyes of hers. She smiled, and my world lit up like a gigantic light bulb.

Later, when we walked out of the hall against the tide of friendly jibes and jealous mumblings from my mates, she grasped my hand like a gentle vice. We didn't go down behind the bull pen to join the groping couples. We realised that this was more than just a one-night stand. It was something special. Instead, we walked, fingers entwined, down the gravel lane. We passed the dairy where the aroma of milk and detergent momentarily robbed me of the French perfume her mother had let her use.

At the tractor shed, where the International and Farmall were locked inside, I attempted a joke by saying, 'I wonder if machines ever have dreams about falling in love.'

'And if they do,' she added, 'I wonder if they come true like our dreams.'

We perched on the piggery fence. The stench was almost forgotten as we chatted like life-long friends. I was surprised by the flow of words that gushed up from somewhere deep inside me. Not once did I fall into my old habit of repeating the lines that one of my film idols had used in winning over a woman. Gone was my shyness. Out came stuff that I'd never even thought about before. Yet it sounded crystal clear like I'd been thinking about it for ages.

She listened intently to all I said. And when she spoke, her words came across with the voice of so much wisdom and experience that they could have almost come from her mother's mouth.

How mature she sounded when she talked about her future. She said she was going to live in Paris, France. At the time my main concern was about learning to live outside the confines of school, let alone a million miles away in some foreign country. But something had already told me that we were meant for a life together. It was only a small fib when I said I'd always planned to live in Paris as a writer. We went on to discuss children. She wanted two boys and a girl. We even agreed on their names: François, Pierre and Michelle.

Then, as we looked into the heavens choosing our love star, she spoke of how she could make her spirit leave her body, how it could travel vast distances. She even said that she'd been to Paris and floated above the Eiffel Tower.

The thought of someone leaving their own body gave me the heebie-jeebies. I changed the conversation quick-smart by asking if she minded if I smoked. She didn't. So I dug out my second-to-last cigarette butt from its hiding place in my sock. I lit it and blew smoke rings out into the night. They would have formed perfect circles if a breeze hadn't been blowing.

When I'd finished my herb, I drew her close. She didn't resist. She whispered something in French. '*Très bon*', I think it was. She shut her eyes, opened her lips slightly, then waited for me to make my move. For a fleeting moment the thought crossed my mind that she might have been around a bit. But I melted into her French kiss and into her taste, which reminded me of the lush creamy smell of a poddy calf.

We finally strolled back to the dance, and she proudly wore my school tie draped loosely around her neck. I was so taken by this blatant act of union that I didn't give a damn about being reported for un-school-like behaviour.

As always, the last dance of the evening was the Slow Waltz. Suddenly my feet worked. Those many years of awkward shuffle vanished. Together we floated through the dimmed lights as if we were so in tune that everything and anything was possible.

Paris, France

Her name was Rita Spargo. She lived five miles away in Yanco township. She went to Leeton High School. Her Dad was a shearer. Her Mum was born in Paris, France.

Never before had so many of my hopes, dreams and aspirations been wrapped up in one single human being. I carried her faded school photograph in my shirt pocket above my heart. Under my pillow I kept strands of her fine auburn hair. Her gift of a pencil sharpener in the shape of the Eiffel Tower was all a budding writer like myself needed for inspiration.

But after that first romantic night, when we'd clung to each other like the sole survivors of a shipwreck, I feared that Rita's love was on the wane.

Due to my impending final exams and the isolation of school, we'd only been able to date once since we'd met. As our relationship drifted into its second month, her love letters had become less frequent and the cakes she smuggled out were getting soggier.

Still, nothing prepared me for what was to happen next. A letter arrived in Rita's handwriting. Hoping to see pages of love hearts, hugs and kisses I ripped it open. There, in black and white, were written the words:

> *Last Saturday Jack Hendersen took me out on a date. We went to the footy in his brand new car then he took me out to the Chinese restaurant for dinner. It was* très bon.

I was devastated.

No amount of sympathy from my mates could help. We all knew Jack Hendersen. He'd been a bitter sports opponent of ours throughout his years at Leeton High before he'd left school and got a job on the packing line at the Leeton Cannery. He played dirty before leaving school; he still did.

Then one day, while I was clutching the Eiffel Tower pencil sharpener trying to project horrible thoughts about Jack Hendersen into Rita's brain, fate intervened.

Ten Quid was at that moment telling us about the German Army's entry into Paris, France. In my hand I held the Eiffel Tower, which was situated in Paris, France. Rita's Mum was born in Paris, France. Rita was fascinated by anything to do with Paris, France. Wiz Watson had once read in my cards that in a past life I'd been beheaded during the French Revolution in Paris, France.

I couldn't work out what all these signs meant. They just didn't add up to anything, didn't make sense. Then, as I was shaking my head in bewilderment, my eyes fell on Jug making detailed notes in his history text book.

Jug was never the studious type, or 'dag' as we called them, so I took a closer look. And there, sandwiched between the two world wars was the weekend race form guide. When Jug saw me peering over his shoulder he leaned back to display the greyhound races at Leeton.

'Hottest tip'a the year,' he whispered.

And right before my very eyes, Jug's finger was pointing at a greyhound racing in the fourth.

It's name – 'Paris, France'.

Never before had the forces of life shone so brightly from the direction I should follow. More astounding still was that Jug had strong connections with the greyhound. He reckoned that the brother-in-law of the sister of the dog's owner had mentioned quite confidentially that Paris, France was set for the biggest win of her racing career.

That night, after gaining permission to use the telephone, I rang Rita and asked if she'd like to go to the dog races on Saturday. I assumed from her silence that she felt a more exciting offer may be in the air.

It was then that I was forced to play my trump cards. I

promised Rita that after the races I'd shout her out for the night of her life. First we'd have dinner at the Leeton Soldiers' Club, where a French cook had recently started work. Following our meal we'd go to the Roxy Theatre, where Gene Kelly was starring in 'An American in Paris'.

'That would be *très bon*,' she said.

I successfully pleaded with Dad-ak for special leave on the grounds that I had to visit an ailing relative, and all was set.

The following Saturday, armed with a magical French phrase Horny had patiently spent the week teaching me, I bound my entire life's savings in my handkerchief. They totalled one pound five and six pence, which included the pound note my Grandmother had given me in case of dire emergency.

I cadged a lift into Yanco and arrived at Rita's place just after lunch. When she opened her front door I was completely flabbergasted. The way she looked, she could have easily been mistaken for a model right off the front page of a French fashion magazine. It was obvious that I couldn't expect her to walk into Leeton, so I went the whole hog and spent my change on a taxi.

The fourth race was near by the time we arrived at the track. After sneaking in the back way so we didn't have to pay, I made an excuse about having to go to the toilet. Instead, I slipped around to the bookies' ring. Thankfully no one else had been tipped off about Paris, France. Her price was holding steady at 18/1.

I glanced through the opposition. From Dingo Pup, the 250/1 long shot, right through to Ted's Choice, the favourite, they had dead-pan names apart from Paris, France. With this, any fleeting idea I may have had of an each way bet was put aside. I decided to put all my money on the win only.

'A quid on the nose, Paris, France,' I spruiked at the bookie. As he scribbled on the betting card I mused that, with my winnings, I'd even be able to buy Rita a friendship ring to show the world, and Jack Hendersen in particular, that she was my sweetheart and no one else's.

But – 'speak of the devil' – when I returned to Rita there he was. Jack Hendersen himself, as ugly as ever and decked out in a swish suit and tie like he was off to visit the Queen.

'G'day Swampy,' Jack spat through his gold fillings.

'G'day Hendo,' I hissed back at him through the gap in my front teeth.

Hendo and I stood almost toe to toe trading 'pooses'. The air around us crackled with tension. The meaner he eyed me, the meaner I eyed him back. When I'd reached the limits of my mean looks, it suddenly struck me that Hendo was just warming to the task. To stave off a humiliating defeat I flung my arm around Rita and pulled her close.

'See ya later Hendo,' I snarled, and led Rita out of harm's way down to the winning post to watch the race.

The instant the boxes sprang open I knew it was my lucky day. Paris, France was every bit the winner. When the field settled down she positioned herself nicely, and pulled out to overtake the leaders as they rounded the bend into the straight. Half way down the straight she hit the lead. With twenty yards to go she had a good four lengths break. With ten yards to go, the race was in the bag.

Where Dingo Pup came from, I wouldn't have a clue. In three strides she collared Paris, France and flashed past to take out the race.

I felt like I'd been bowled over by a diesel locomotive.

I don't know how long I stood there staring blankly out into space. It just wouldn't sink in, not even after the track commentator announced that Dingo Pup had beaten Paris, France by a long neck. When I finally turned to Rita, I could tell she knew what had happened.

She took it well, given the circumstances. Far better than I did really. She bought a pie for us to share and we sat on the cold concrete steps amongst the torn betting tickets and sauce-stained wrappers.

'This tastes *très bon*,' she said.

I knew she was only trying to revive my shattered spirits.

The pie could have easily passed as a couple of slabs of frozen boot leather with slimy gunk inside. Still, I mumbled agreement and forced my half down so as not to offend her.

When we'd finished eating, Rita asked if I minded whether she went in search of Hendo to see if he'd drive us back to her place. I knew he wouldn't miss out on an opportunity like that. No bloke in his right mind would. What did surprise me, though, was the way Rita willingly sat in the back seat of Hendo's new Vanguard and held my hand all the way back to Yanco.

After Hendo dropped us off, he went and parked just down the road. Rita and I stood at her front gate. I'd have been happy to stay there until eternity holding onto those soft white hands. But after a few minutes I noticed that her eyes began to wander in the direction of Hendo's car and something told me that she may have wanted a bit more out of life than to hang around a rusty old gate with a bloke who'd just lost his last penny.

Then the magical French phrase Horny had taught me came to mind. He'd said the words worked like a romantic potion, rendering females helpless in a bloke's arms.

'*Je t'aime*. I love you,' I blurted.

And Rita leaned over and kissed me so gently that little electric sparks sprung up all over my cheek.

'*Au revoir*,' she replied.

Muck-up Day

The Fifth Year's last official day of school was named Muck-up Day. Following that came two weeks of 'stu-vac', personal study time, then D-Day, the Leaving Certificate Exams.

Muck-up Day was traditionally when the retiring Fifth Years let off the steam that had been building up over the years. And if one thing was a dead cert, our escape valves were well and truly primed to blow.

Many of the Muck-up Day pranks had become etched into our folklore over the decades. Jug reckoned that, as far back as the twenties, a bloke by the name of 'Suicide' Smith rode a penny farthing bicycle, while blindfolded, around the top of the school's one-hundred-and-fifty foot high concrete water tower.

'The mob watchin' below was agape, wonder'n' just how crazy Suicide really was,' Jug related. 'It was a disaster waitin' ta happen. Everyone knew that, 'cept Suicide. That was till 'is third time round when the bike got the wobbles 'n over 'e went.'

Luck was apparently with Suicide that day because when he fell, he fell inward, not outward. Being blindfolded, he wasn't immediately aware of his good fortune. For that split second before splashdown he believed he was headed toward certain death on the ground far below.

'An' that's why, thirty or so years later, there's still that crook taint in the water supply,' Jug said.

1932 was the year the Fifth Years let the stud Hereford bull loose amongst the Jersey and Guernsey dairy herd.

'They reckon,' Jug said, 'that when the bull was at last dragged out from the cows' paddock, it 'ad a smile on its face so wide, ya could see its back molars. Fair dinkum!'

Enjoyable as the experience may have been for the bull, the

consequences of that particular prank were to have dramatic and long lasting effects on the school's dairy breeding program.

Then there was the year the Fifth Years broke into the cadet store. They armed themselves with .303 rifles and blanks, and surrounded the teacher's quarters. Their idea was to put the wind up the Nits.

It worked.

The first shots were fired on the stroke of midnight. Before the second hand had moved, every Nit in the teachers' quarters was under his bed.

'They reckon the windows started ta rattle 'cause the Nits were shakin' so much. Then back in me brotha's year,' Jug said, ''is mob took over the school block. Joe says it was like a siege, jus' like the ones ya hear 'bout on the wireless, only bigger. 'Ventually the Nits joined up with the farm staff ta storm the place. Joe reckoned they 'ad a huge stoush. But the Fifth Years were outnumbered.'

It almost went without saying that, when it came to organising our Muck-up Day activities, Jug wanted to go one better than his brother and close the school block until at least after recess. Before anyone else could get a word in, Jug was dishing out orders like they were cards in a poker game.

Slimy, 'Battler' Britton and a couple of others were put in charge of kicking the day off with as much confusion as possible. Their job was to nick the donger out of the wake-up bell and disconnect the siren outside the staff room.

Another group, led by Bluey and 'Mottley' Green, broke into the science lab and got busy making phosphorus balls. By early morning these tiny explosives had been spread throughout the school. There they waited for their unsuspecting victims to tread on them and set them off.

Jug, me, Shorty Sargent and some others organised the tucker.

'An army marches on its stomach,' Jug announced. Then added, ''N this is gonna to be all out war!'

It took us three sorties into the kitchen to gather enough

bread, butter, jam, plus the two bags of flour we needed to make flour bombs.

Before daybreak we'd well and truly settled into the second storey of the class block. Meat and Horny arrived back from their activities leading Buttercup, the Jersey cow. Up the steps they came.

'Gotta 'ave fresh milk with me cuppa, eh Buttercup?' Meat said to the reluctant cow.

After a slap-up breakfast, we started making the weaponry needed if we were going to hold the enemy at bay. By the time the wake-up bell should have rung, confusion ran rife in the dorms. Nits crept nervously from one patch of exploding phosphorus balls to the next, attempting to get the kids up and going.

By school time, bedlam reigned supreme.

We'd locked the main doors into the class block and taken up positions at the windows overlooking the quadrangle. From there, we bombarded anyone who tried to enter with flour and water bombs. By 9.30 the Nits had beaten a retreat to the far side of the quadrangle. We brazenly lit herbs and blew smoke out of the windows. When Slimy dropped his dacks and flashed his bare bum, the students cheered at his utter disrespect for authority.

By recess the mood in our camp was electric. We were almost drunk on our new-found power. We swore at the Nits. 'Ape, go to hell!' we chanted. We made finger signs and screwed up our faces. Buttercup even got into the spirit of things. She brought howls of laughter and applause when she stuck her head out the staff-room window and let out a loud bellow.

We held the entire school at our mercy. We'd beaten Joe's record. Jug was almost in tears. This was his finest hour. It was *our* finest hour. No other group had so completely and utterly shut down the school. We felt as if we could have stayed there until eternity. No one or nothing could stop us!

Then Dad-ak appeared.

As he strode out from Mutch House, down along the path

past the water bubblers, kids and Nits scampered out of his way. Across the quadrangle he came. A hush fell over the place. We could almost see the steam hissing out of his ears, the fire in his eyes.

Jug turned to Meat: 'Let 'im 'ave it!'

Meat lit up with the challenge.

After having been caned more times than any other student in the recorded history of Yanco Ag, we knew how much Meat wanted revenge. Now the tables were turned. Dad-ak was at his mercy. Meat took a flour bomb in his right hand. He lifted it into throwing position. We held our breath as Dad-ak came within range.

'Now!' Jug urged. 'Now!'

For some strange reason, Meat decided not to go through with it. He seemed to baulk. Maybe he lost his nerve. Maybe he felt sorry for Dad-ak. I don't know. But at the last moment, he put aside the flour bomb.

We heard the doors being unlocked as Dad-ak entered the school block. Up the stairs he came, his keys jangling like a snapped chain.

In an attempt to display a united front, we jostled for position behind Buttercup. Then somehow I got shoved to the fore. My heart was beating so hard that I could feel my eyeballs pounding in their sockets. Someone was breathing heavily down the back of my neck. It might have been Buttercup. Dad-ak reached the top of the stairs. He spun around the corner. Then he stopped.

I looked at him, down at the far end of the corridor.

He looked back at me.

I looked at him.

He looked at me.

He looked real angry. Not just normal old angry. But real, mean, angry angry; more angry than I'd ever seen him look. The picture came into my head of a group of petrified gazelles cornered by a raging lion. We were the gazelles. Dad-ak was the lion. What's more, he was about to rip us to shreds.

A finger jabbed into my back.

'Say somethin',' Jug whispered.

A few faint grunts confirmed I was to be the group's spokesman. Panic set in. I couldn't think. I went blank.

'Say somethin'.'

I opened up my mouth.

'Hello,' I said, real meek and mild.

Custer's Last Stand

It had to happen. You can't stop the inevitable. You can't turn back the hands of time to delay something as important as the Leaving Certificate Exams. You can't say 'Look, I've mucked this up! Let's start again so I can have another bash.'

Life's not like that.

It wasn't as if I hadn't been given enough warning. All during fifth year the Nits had kept up a sustained barrage of: 'You must study hard boys. Your entire future rests on the outcome of these exams.' Perhaps I'd switched off. That wasn't unusual, especially when the words came from a Nit. If they'd said, 'Now this is the way to bowl a wrong-un',' my attention would have stuck to them like clay to a disc plough.

But cricket wasn't what it was about.

The two weeks of stu-vac began in a panic that never waned. It was like a cement mixer was churning in my stomach. Still, I gave it my best: dagged like I'd never dagged before, burnt the midnight oil by the gallon. If it had been possible to tear the pages out of my text books, scrunch them up and infuse them into my brain, I'd have done it. I'd have done anything. And the pressure began to tell, not only on me, but also on my mates. It was written on their faces; etched in those first signs of impending doom.

Then tragedy.

We knew Meat had been worried about the exams. He'd gone real quiet, right into his shell.

'You okay mate?' Jug had asked him.

'Don't know, Jug. I reckon somethin's goin' wrong in me brain,' he'd replied. 'I jus' can't seem ta think proper, no more.'

'Well Meat, it's probably just some sort'a minor mechanical problem like ya drive shaft or somethin',' Jug had chided.

'Whatcha mean by that, Jug?' Meat had asked, full of concern. We'd laughed at him.

But we didn't laugh when Meat disappeared. We knew something terrible was happening, something far more serious than a minor mechanical problem. We searched high and low for him, but to no avail. It wasn't until around dawn that a First Year on Dairy Stock discovered him behind the silos.

Never had I seen so much fright in anyone's eyes as I saw in Meat's that morning. They were cracked open in a glassy stare that reminded me of a rabbit's eyes when it's caught in the steel jaws of a trap.

'I can't do it, Jug,' Meat blubbered. 'I'm scared. I really want'a be somethin' ya know. I wanna be better'n a butcher like me dad. But I don't reckon I got the brains, Jug. I jus' don't reckon I got the brains no more.'

That incident shook us all up. It made me realise just how much I'd been involved in trying to save my own skin, rather than being on hand to help a mate in need. What's more, Meat was the sort of bloke who would have been the first in line to help any of us. We all knew that. He'd done it before, many times.

After we finally settled Meat back into bed, we went into Jug's dagging hole, where he removed the false back on his locker. There lay our gang's herb stash; 'the treasury' we called it. To me, Jug's had been an amazing feat. He had achieved everything he set out to do way back in first year. He'd captured the cigarette monopoly of the school and become the owner of the kitchen keys. He was king-pin. Everyone knew that, even Mottley Green the School Captain. If anyone wanted anything done, they went straight to Jug. They knew that he could make things happen around the place that no one else could; things that a lot of people weren't too keen on seeing happen.

For once, however, Jug was anything but cock-a-hoop with his own efforts.

'Five years'a bloody 'ard slog,' he lamented, ''n soon they're not gonna be worth a brass razoo. They reckon herbs bloody well kill ya' anyway.'

With exam fever well and truly setting in, each of us handled it differently. Slimy's dagging hole started to look like a lucky charms junk shop. Jug stopped thinking about sex and chucked in smoking and gambling. Bluey got a crazy idea about fish. He'd read somewhere that it was 'brain food'.

'It sharpens the mind,' he reckoned.

'What's ya proof?' Jug challenged him.

'Have ya ever met a dumb Eskimo?'

That stumped us. We'd never even seen an Eskimo. Still, it didn't matter to Bluey. He got stuck into the sardines like they were going out of style. He devoured can after can. Within a week he stank so badly that the stray cats started hanging around his dagging hole.

I didn't miss out either. Exam fever clobbered me. It began in earnest when I had a nightmare about being in heaps of strife. I was on detention, cleaning the dunnies after a footy carnival. The stench was so vile that I was struggling to hold back from spewing. And there was Dad-ak, handkerchief covering his face, yelling at the top of his voice, 'You'd better get used to this job son, because the way you're going it's all you'll ever amount to!'

The more I tried to snatch back those wasted hours of late night card games and turn them into study, the more I felt I was losing the battle. It was painfully obvious that I'd gone about the whole of my schooling the wrong way.

Then it struck me. It was as if all the lights had snapped on, almost like a visitation. My only hope was divine intervention. Who else could produce miracles?

I took to religion. I became a true believer. I learnt the Lord's Prayer off by heart. It took two days, but I did it. For the first time in ages things began to look brighter. But then I started thinking that perhaps God's miracles didn't come with guarantees, not even to true believers. To cover myself I took to eating sardines. I quit smoking and gambling; collected lucky charms.

And if thoughts of sex entered my mind, I closed my eyes and tried to recall the first twenty elements of the Periodic Table.

My waking hours were spent trying to cram as much as possible into the vacuum of my skull. So were my sleeping hours. I began to take up Joe's old way of dagging, the one that almost got him into university.

'I call it the "Joe Ashton Absorption Method'a Study", Swamp. A few scientistic fellers are pretty keen on it too,' Joe had told me.

Each night before bed, Joe reckoned he used to place his text books under his pillow. The theory was that while he slept the knowledge from the books seeped through his pillow and was absorbed into his brain.

'It works somethin' like os-most-is, Swamp.'

Night after night I stacked text books under my pillow. But while the technique may have almost got Joe into university, all I got was a crook neck.

On D-Day, the morning of the exams, the horror continued for Meat. He woke up and his mind had gone blank.

'Let's face it Jug, I ain't got no brains in me head at all. I'm just bloody dumb. As simple as that.'

The poor bloke could hardly remember his own name. Meat might not have been the brightest bloke on earth, but there was one thing that he couldn't have been labelled, and that was a bludger. When it came to the crunch, Meat always gave it his best shot. But that morning he broke down completely. Jug and I even had to help him shower and dress.

After breakfast I returned to my dagging hole and gathered my pen, ink, blotting paper, pencils, rubbers and ruler. My time was up. The inevitable had arrived and I headed down to the school hall to face the Leaving Certificate Exams.

In the final minutes before the doors opened we milled around outside smoking cigarettes. I felt like I was living in a film. I started to think about 'Little Big Horn', where General Custer and his men were wiped out by Big Chief Sitting Bull and his braves in that historic battle.

And as I sucked in a velvet veil of cigarette smoke I had visions of that fateful day. I could picture it so clearly, like I was living it. Me, the preacher, clutching for dear life onto my tiny Gideon's Bible, silently mumbling the Lord's Prayer. Jug, as General Custer, fronting a brave face until the very end. Private Meat, slumped on the steps of the hall, sobbing. Lieutenant Bluey, surrounded by whingeing cats. The rest of the troops exhausted, even before the final battle began.

No amount of pre-planning could have prepared us for this. Fate had led us here. There was no turning back; no avenue of escape. There we were, sixteen, seventeen years of age, the oldest we'd ever been, waiting in pensive silence for the Indians to arrive and finish us off.

Empty Pockets

My last night at Yanco Ag was spent on Horn Beach. For our final fling, we organised a beach party just like we'd seen in the flicks, without the girls of course. Just us blokes.

In five years of schooling, it was the first time I'd broken the rule about always sleeping in dorms or dagging holes. But I was openly flouting authority by then; we all were. With the Leaving Certificate Exams behind us, we were pumped up with the spirit of freedom. We were ready to fly; ready to take on the outside world.

At the beach we gathered a stack of dry wood and lit a bonfire. In a symbolic gesture, we tossed most of our old school clothes and books onto the flames. We whooped and hollered like a crazy pack of Wild West Indians. But after our stuff had turned to cinders and the fire died down, we went much the same way.

No one seemed in the mood for celebrations. Even the bottle of Barossa Pearl sat untouched. I tried to start a sing-along to get some pep into the evening, but that night the harmonica had a forlorn feel about it. Its sounds rebounded off the mudbanks like a lamented cry.

'For Christ's sake Swampy, shut that bloody thing up will ya?' Jug snapped.

That stung. I'd known Jug to get angry before. But not like that. And never with me. There was real bitterness in his voice.

'Sorry mate,' he said after I'd put the harmonica away. 'I jus' got lots on me plate, that's all.'

I understood. In the end we all just sat, staring long and hard into the fire, sniffing at the breeze off the Murrumbidgee River, that one last time.

Mum and Dad had moved from Beckom, so I had no real place to call home. Unlike most of my mates there wasn't a family farm for me to return to. There were no childhood friends waiting to greet me by saying, 'Hey! Great to see ya back ta stay, we're lookin' for a good wicketkeeper'.

At school I'd always been too keen on the company of others to have knuckled down and lived the more solitary life of a dag. My school work had slipped. University and teachers college were out of the question, and with the rural crisis at hand it was unlikely I'd get a decent job on the land.

The thought came over me of trying to find work in a city like Sydney. I'd been there once and hadn't liked it one iota. Those huge department stores full of life-size fashion dummies gawked at me like I was out of place, when it was they who were the odd ones out. They were the ones without hearts, or souls, or brains in their head.

Everywhere I'd gone I'd been jostled by hordes of people, and not a single one of them would give a country bumpkin like me the time of day. And the way they spoke – they spat their words as if they were always in a rush, leaving me gazing up at the skyscrapers, still confused as to where the hell Pitt Street could be.

The days since the final exams had been chaotic. We'd been busy trying to sell off our gang's assets for hard cash. The money we'd made from our herb stash was disappointing. We hadn't looked like bagging as much as we'd hoped from the sale of our collection of keys to the kitchen either.

Then Jug had a brainwave.

The morning before we went to Horn Beach, he cadged a lift into Leeton, where he got a stack of keys made from our copies. That afternoon he sold the keys to different gangs, along with a guarantee that the particular key they'd purchased was the only copy in existence. We could imagine the bedlam in the kitchen after midnight as the rival gangs stumbled over each other, all with exactly the same keys.

Thanks to Jug's idea, we struck it rich. 'Rolling in it,' as Meat said. And we were too; that was until Jug talked us into buying a parcel of shares in an oil company Joe had just acquired an interest in. Joe had estimated that we'd make at least a 1,000 per cent profit from our investment, just as soon as they struck oil.

'These shares are our gang's legacy ta the future and Meat's guarantee of a job,' Jug declared while taking our money back.

Jug's master plan was that, after we'd made our killing on the stockmarket, we'd buy a cattle station. A place where we could all live together. Still, even with such grand hopes and promises, I don't think I'd have parted with my dough so readily if it hadn't been for Meat's welfare. Over the years I'd lost a lot on Joe's hare-brained schemes. I was still pretty shirty about what happened the week before, when he'd written giving Jug and me the hot gossip on a horse that a mate was entering in a maiden at Randwick.

Joe had described the nag as 'the next Phar Lap'. With a gigantic rap like that I'd laid out the spending money Mum and Dad had sent for my three-day train trip home. As it turned out, the horse came from Melbourne, where it'd been trained to run in an anti-clockwise direction. On its Sydney debut it couldn't handle going around the track the opposite way and had just about pulled its jockey clean back over the border into Victoria.

The morning after Horn Beach, we returned to school for breakfast, where Rock-Jaw gave his annual Fifth Year farewell speech on behalf of the Nits and students. We'd never got on too well with Rock-Jaw, not that we'd done anything wrong to him personally. We actually tried to ignore him as best we could. But he had aspirations of becoming a Headmaster like Dad-ak. He liked things to run in a strict, manageable order. Even though he said the usual guff about how we'd be missed and how everyone wished us well, Rock-Jaw's words somehow seemed to lack that heartfelt sentiment of his previous farewell speeches.

After breakfast we returned to our dorms to say cheerio to the kids we'd been Prefects to. Thankfully, I'd had a good dorm. Blokes like 'Hair', 'Eggy', 'Baa', 'Cracker' and 'Smelly'. Real little characters. They weren't ratbags like some of the kids in the other dorms. For a parting gift they'd chipped in and bought me a pewter beer mug, inscribed with the words:

Have a few for us.
From all your Second Year mates.

When the siren rang for them to go to class, I pulled down my dagging hole and cleaned out what little remained from my locker. Finally I squeezed into my school uniform. Because I had a train to catch, I was the first called into Dad-ak's office to hear his final words of advice and worldly wisdom.

Dad-ak's office held many memories for me. None of them too good. Just standing there gave me a sense of being in trouble. I could almost hear the ring of angry words and the swish of the cane, feel the stinging sensation on my fingers.

'Well, son,' Dad-ak said, 'you're certainly not the brightest kid that's gone through Yanco Ag.'

It took a tick to realise that it was me he was talking to. Dad-ak had never called me 'son' before. On a good day it might have been 'you silly galah'. From there it often plummeted to the depths of 'you brainless twit' – even worse when I got into real strife. A *lot* worse!

But in an odd, friendly manner Dad-ak asked if I had any plans for the future.

'Not really, Sir.'

Dad-ak looked concerned. Then, almost as if he was weighing up my life's options, he advised me to give away football. He reckoned that I ran like a 'Scandinavian Trotting Duck' and that I'd lose my head in a high tackle one day.

'Stick with cricket,' he said, 'and keep writing those little stories of yours. Some are quite humorous. You never know where they'll lead.'

'Yes Sir.'

And that, I thought, with more than a touch of relief, was going to be the end of it. But when it came to our parting handshake, Dad-ak seized onto me almost as if he didn't want to let go. His fingernails dug into the back of my hand. He latched onto my shoulder. As we stood there, awkwardly facing each other, he caught me off-guard.

'In life, son,' he blurted, 'we're given just a pocketful of opportunities. You, I'm afraid, have a near-empty pocket, so you'd better use what's there to the utmost of your ability.'

Although I'd never swear to it, in the emotion of that moment, I thought I saw the faintest hint of mist coming to Dad-ak's eyes.

'Yes Sir,' I replied. Then, to save further embarrassment, I freed myself from his grasp and hurriedly turned on my heels.

As I reached the door, I started to choke up. I was hit with the overwhelming compulsion to apologise for all the trouble I'd caused over the years. More than anything, I wanted to bare my soul to that monolith of strength, discipline and authority who, before my eyes, had almost shown signs of human frailty.

I wanted to own up that it'd been me who'd set Brutus free at the Leeton Show where he'd run amuck through the Chad Morgan concert. I wanted to confess to having thrown the penny bungers on his roof after cracker night, back in Third Year. That I'd been the one who'd gone around in the dead of the night dipping kids' hands in warm water, causing them to wet their beds. That it had started out as a harmless prank and that no one, least of all me, expected it to turn into hysteria, with kids thinking they were dying from some foreign bladder disease.

I'd been no saint. I knew that. I'd given as good as I'd got. There were other things that I wanted to own up to. Lots of things. And I would have, too, but when I heard Dad-ak blowing his nose, I thought better of it and walked out the door.

Jug had just arrived outside. He was slouching against the

wall, acting as cool as a cucumber. When he noticed I was teary his look of confidence changed.

'How was it?' Jug whispered.

I gave a wince of agony, then tucked my hands under my armpits as if I'd just been given the caning of my life.

'Pure hell,' I hissed.

In memory of

'Hippie' Payne

'Hackie' Plant

'Mangle-dog' Davidson

. . . those of us who haven't made it this far.

WAKEFIELD PRESS

This Is My Friend's Chair

Geraldine Halls

'In a world of relentless hype and 15-minute fame, I am wary of lavishing the superlatives on this book; they would only diminish it.'

Tony Baker, *Advertiser*

This beautifully paced saga, told through the eyes of Sophie Conway, spans forty years from the early twenties to the sixties. Set between Adelaide and London, it is a story of family life, betrayals and reconciliations, conveyed by a series of vignettes, finely crafted dialogues, and subtly manipulated variations in time and mood. Sophie's love-hate relationship with Lizzie Grey, the 'intruder in the Conway family' forms a constant thread in this epic drama of a family's decline and disintegration.

ISBN 1 86254 342 9   RRP $19.95

WAKEFIELD PRESS

Bringing the Water

New writing from South Australia
Edited by Moya Costello and Barry Westburg

Thirty-five stories flow through *Bringing the Water*, a collection of 'grass roots' writing from people living in the driest state of the driest continent in the world.

ISBN 1 86254 312 7   RRP $14.95

WAKEFIELD PRESS

Black Horse Odyssey

Search for the lost city of Rome in China
David Harris

This intriguing book tells the story of David Harris's search for archaeological evidence of a city built 1200 kilometres south-west of Beijing thirteen centuries before Marco Polo 'discovered' China for the western world.

ISBN 1 86254 270 8   RRP $12.95

No Bed of Roses

Memoirs of a Madam
Patti Walkuski and David Harris

No Bed of Roses is an intimate, often horrifying, account of an abused girl's transformation into a powerful madam, and the subsequent collapse of her empire.

ISBN 1 86254 310 0   RRP $17.95

WAKEFIELD PRESS

Bonetown

Steve Evans

'Even in the world of the very ordinary, Steve Evans finds extraordinary poetry.'

Peter Goldsworthy

Steve Evans captures life in an Australian country town: lost kites, a car parked in a lake, a road-worker washg with butter. he also applies a feral logic to satellites, snakes and angels, producing an agile and sensuous collection of poetry.

ISBN 1 86254 332 1   RRP $12.95

WAKEFIELD PRESS

The Devil You Know

Frederick Guilhaus

Corruption in the boardroom,
Murder in the wilderness,
A woman's fight for all she believes in . . .

Brady Martin, unemployed and fed up, ignites rebellion among Tasmanian farmers who are being forced off their land by the banks. Meanwhile in Sydney, the directors of a new investment corporation play a dicey game with the nation's superannuation funds.

. . . *The Devil You Know* is a thriller-romance for the nineties.

ISBN 1 96254 341 0   RRP $18.95

WAKEFIELD PRESS

Trees In My Ears

Children from around the world
talk to Christine Harris
Christine Harris

Christine Harris travelled in Italy, Turkey, Russia, China and Australia to compile this funny, poignant and provocative book of quotes from children about topics ranging from families and pets to a planet in jeopardy.

ISBN 1 86254 283 X   RRP $14.95

WAKEFIELD PRESS

Wakefield Crime Classics

This series revives forgotten or neglected gems of crime and mystery fiction by Australian authors. Most of the writers, published between the 1920s and 1970s, became international stars, while remaining little known in Australia. Several of the novels are being published in Australia for the first time.

PATRICIA CARLON
The Souvenir: A guessproof whodunnit
ISBN 1 86254 294 5 $12.95
The Whispering Wall: Lethal house, silent witness, talking wall
ISBN 1 86254 280 5 $12.95

S.H. COURTIER
Death in Dreamtime: A mystery of masks and ciphers
ISBN 1 86254 295 3 $12.95
Ligny's Lake: The race to solve the riddles of a vanishing man
ISBN 1 86254 286 4 $12.95

PAT FLOWER
Vanishing Point: Where intimacy turns to violence
ISBN 1 86254 292 9 $12.95

ARTHUR GASK
The Secret of the Garden: Criminal? Surgeon? Jockey? Friend?
ISBN 1 86254 291 0 $12.95

CHARLOTTE JAY
Arms for Adonis: Blood and love in Lebanon
ISBN 1 86254 296 1 $14.95
Beat Not the Bones: A tale of terror in the tropics
ISBN 1 86254 287 2 $12.95
A Hank of Hair: An exquisite danse macabre
ISBN 1 86254 289 9 $12.95

A.E. MARTIN
Common People: Murder in sideshow alley
ISBN 1 86254 303 8 $14.95
The Misplaced Corpse: Introducing Rosie Bosanky, alarming, disarming and altogether charming
ISBN 1 86254 281 3 $12.95
Sinners Never Die: A savage small-town saga
ISBN 1 86254 290 2 $12.95

WAKEFIELD PRESS

Wakefield Press has been publishing good Australian books for over fifty years. For a catalogue of current and forthcoming titles, or to add your name to our mailing list, send your name and address to:

Wakefield Press, Box 2266, Kent Town, South Australia 5071.

TELEPHONE (08) 362 8800   FAX (08) 362 7592